I0552230

IGEN

Forgotten Worlds, Volume 7

Prudence MacLeod

Published by Prudence MacLeod, 2023.

IGEN

by

Prudence MacLeod

This is a work of fiction. Similarities to real people, places, or events are entirely coincidental.

IGEN

First edition. November 29, 2023.

ISBN: 978-1927478295

Written by Prudence MacLeod.

A Puzzle

"Floo, are you certain?"

"I am, Eelee, see here? It's outside Igen right now."

"Are you sure, I see only a flashing point of light darting about."

"That's how this is supposed to work, Eelee, the flashing light speaks of an object outside Igen. See how fast it moves, and changes direction to stay close? The original purpose of Igen has been served, the great question answered, they do exist, and we have been found."

"Floo, what can we do?"

"Pray they can't find a way in, or that the Gants don't let them in."

"And if they do?"

"Kill them before they kill us." Slowly she nodded her head in agreement, he was right she knew, he always was. "We need to get out of here; I hear the Gants coming. We don't want to be caught in the open light." Together they sprinted away.

* * * * *

Admiral Jeannie Sorenson stood on the bridge of the starship Reacher, the last home of humanity and a few other species. The admiral was one of only twenty SUVI, a species of mutated humans, and at this point her agile mind was completely intrigued. "Sorenson to EX2, report."

Her call was answered by the captain of the explorer ship EX2, a woman of the Earalith, one of only a dozen still in existence. "Morthel here, Admiral. It's definitely a ship, extremely old, moving under the momentum gained sometime in the past. There are hundreds, perhaps thousands, of life signs on board, but Thirteen believes them to be feral."

"Feral?"

"Their movements are more like hunting or grazing animals, no stationary activity on what we believe to be the bridge, or near the main power source, nor anywhere near the main engines which have gone cold."

"Gone cold?"

"We believe it was originally nuclear powered, Admiral. It has another power source maintaining atmosphere and some other vital systems."

"Any response to hails?"

"None, Admiral."

"Docking ports?"

"We found several, all locked tight."

"Come home, Morthel. We need to put our heads together."

"Aye, Admiral, coming home." With that the agile explorer ship turned and shot away from the massive object and back toward the Reacher.

* * * * *

As usual, Admiral Sorenson was pacing while the others assembled in the Reacher's briefing room. Finally, everyone arrived and settled into a chair. "All ships captains and passenger representatives present, Admiral."

"Thank you, Vice Admiral Drake." Jeannie smiled then took her seat at the head of the table. "All right, people, we have a bit of a puzzle on our hands. Five days ago, the Maccay observers on the Kreenon picked something up on sensors about halfway between systems. By the time we realized it was artificial and got the fleet stopped, we'd overshot it by a couple of days.

"We backtracked and located the object then EX2 went out for a look. Captain Morthel, report."

"The object is a ship, Admiral," replied Morthel. "It's roughly the size of the Reacher, traveling mainly on momentum gained sometime in the past. Its main nuclear engines are cold, but it has a secondary power source still functioning. There are a large number of life signs aboard, but we believe them to be feral. We tried hailing them with every language in Linsey's database but received no answer."

"Feral? How did you reach that conclusion?" asked Miriam Holbrooke, President of the Passengers Association.

"SUVI Thirteen came to that conclusion after observing the movements of the life signs," replied Morthel. "A working ship will have a number of stationary life signs, people working at stations like sensors, etc. We found no such stationary signs. Instead, what we could see looked to Thirteen like herds of animals and hunters stalking them."

"I see, that does make sense, and he would understand what he was seeing."

Jeannie chuckled at that. "So, friends and family, what do we have here? Any ideas?"

It was Olga Volkov, captain of the salvage ship, Recovery One, who spoke first, addressing her comment to Jeannie's grandfather, Captain Baris of Recovery Two. "What do you think, Frank, a generation ship?"

"Sounds like it all right," he replied.

"All right, you two, what the heck is a generation ship?" asked Jeannie.

"It's a sub-lightspeed starship," replied Captain Baris. "There was a plan on Earth to build several of them before the star drive was invented. Once the faster engines were discovered the ships were converted to colonist transports.

"A generation ship is the only way to explore the galaxy if you don't have star drive. Your crew sets out on a journey to a nearby star system, but it will be their descendants who actually arrive at the destination.

"As the crew ages they have to educate and train their children to take over. The hope was to preserve the species and explore the galaxy, even though those who built the ship would never see an alien planet."

"I see," mused Jeannie. "Okay, so if that's what this object is, what do we have here, what could have gone wrong? Speculate, people."

"Could be anything, Admiral," said Olga, "mutiny, disease, anything. It's old, and if those engines just ran down then it's really old. A lot of generations could have come and gone in that length of time. Perhaps the technical knowledge to operate the ship was lost slowly over that span of time, the passengers and crew sinking back into barbarism."

"Okay, so what do we do here?"

"Admiral, if we don't investigate, I could have a mutiny on my ship," sighed Captain Ka'Ron of the Morar ship, Kreenon. "Those curious Maccay will drive the rest of us to madness."

Jeannie chuckled at that. "They truly are a curious people. Well, Ka'Ron wants to take a closer look, anybody else?"

"There might be another language or two on that ship that I could add to my database," grinned Captain Linsey da Silva, captain of the fleet's diplomat ship and Chief of Interspecies Relations.

Captain Sessas was the next to speak. Sessas, a Saurian woman for whom verbal speech is difficult, communicating mainly through a translation device created by Linsey da Silva, had risen from rescued slave to captain of the fleet's rescue ship, Retriever. She has a keen mind and is well respected by all the captains.

"Sessas curious, but wary. Sessas think Admiral curious too."

Jeannie chuckled at that. "Yes, I am, Sessas, and yet wary also. All right, we'll take a closer look. Admiral Sorenson to Probie."

"Probie is here, Admiral. There is a task for Probie?"

"Yes, my friend, there is. Outside the Reacher is another ship of unknown origins. I want you to launch and thoroughly investigate. I want to know everything you can learn about this ship."

"Probie is launching."

"The probe is away, Admiral, chuckled Captain Rhonda Moore of the Reacher, looking up from her info pad."

"All right, folks, get some rest then we'll meet here again first thing tomorrow to see what Probie can tell us." With that the meeting broke up.

* * * * *

"What is it, Tonts? Have they returned?"

"Yes, Keta, they have, but I believe there are a lot more of them than we can detect."

"Oh?"

"Yes, just a flicker now and then, but something. I just wish we had one of those intuitive elders here, their intuition would be invaluable."

"Ah yes, but they're only a few left alive, and none who have full command of their faculties. Ah well, what can you do. It was hard enough to train a young Gant before when we knew an attack was coming, now it's nearly impossible, and the world of Igen is failing.

"Do you think the outsiders will help or destroy us?"

Tonts sighed and glanced at the three entrances to the room of power. Seeing no threat, he returned his attention to his companion. "Who knows, our prophecies say it could go either way while the Growes prophecy says they will devour all. Sadly, the answer lies outside."

"Are they trying to find a way into Igen?"

"No, just buzzing about outside for now. We must wait and see; hope for the best."

As Tonts said this last, another stuck his head through one of the entrances. "Growes war party approaching."

"Dammit, Tonts, go," said Keta as she began locking the entrances. He hurried away and Keta locked the door behind her as she joined him. They dare not let the Growes get at the controls of Igen.

* * * * *

With a snarl on his face, Floo released the handle on the unyielding door. "We were so close, Eelee. So close. Did they escape again?"

"Through another opening, yes."

"And now they've sealed us off from the room of controls. They must know of the outsiders and are trying to let them in. Put out the word, every access to Igen must be heavily guarded. All fighters must be involved." She nodded and pointed to another who hurried away to carry the orders to all Growes everywhere in Igen.

* * * * *

"Everyone's here, Admiral."

"Thank you, Vice-Admiral Drake," smiled Jeannie. "Linsey, has Probie reported yet?"

"She has, Admiral. Probie transmitted a steady stream of information to Friendship who then helped me organize much of it so we organics can understand it. Here's the basic breakdown.

"That ship is approximately ten thousand years old, is in bad shape, has a breathable atmosphere, several hull breaches that have been sealed off, and the one power source is failing. The interior is much like a planetary surface in some areas and more a ship like in others. The ship has no shields, weapons, or transporters.

"Probie also observed a small number of life signs gathering on what is believed to be a secondary bridge, but another group chased them off. She also believes that small group was aware of her and her movements. She believes the ship offers no threat to the fleet."

"Well done, Linsey. Tell Probie I said so. All right people, opinions, options?"

"Jeannie, what are we doing here?"

"Grandfather?"

"Why are we here? What are you planning to do? Are we going to pillage that ship?"

Jeannie chuckled at that. "No, Grandfather, we're not turning pirate. At the moment we're deciding if our curiosity has been sufficiently satisfied or not."

"Mine sure isn't," grinned Captain da Silva. "There has to be at least one language over there I can add to the database, and another people to meet and talk to."

Miriam Holbrooke of the Passengers Association sighed elaborately. "Linsey, you're not going to invite them all onto the Reacher, are you? Rhonda will just dump them in my lap." That brought a round of chuckles from all the captains.

"Seriously, Admiral, shouldn't we try to make contact with them, offer some help?" asked the Vice-Admiral.

"EX2 did try, Vice-Admiral," said Captain Morthel. "We got no response."

Jeannie sighed at that. "Speculate on that, people. What are the possible reasons they would not respond?"

"Could be they no longer have the functioning tech," mused Olga Volkov.

"Actually, I expect the other is the most likely reason," said Miriam.

"Miriam?"

"Admiral, you know as well as I do what happens when you have a growing population in a confined space. If we'd been left on Elysium for generations, we'd have outgrown the Caverns, some would be forced outside, others would fight for resources, etc.

"As the generations passed and education deteriorated, those remaining would slowly sink into barbarism, eventually creating a much more primitive society. The fate of the original crew of the Kreenon and their descendants clearly demonstrates this."

"Sadly, you're right, I believe, Miriam," said Jeannie. "I remember and agree, that would have been the fate of the people in the Caverns. So, you believe the people on this generation ship have suffered this fate, they've devolved back to a more primitive society?"

"I think it's quite likely."

"Anyone else?"

"She's probably right, Admiral," agreed Linsey. "Probie reports all the ship's systems are on auto and in need of adjustment or repair. I'd really like to try contacting them again."

"And I'm curious as to where they came from and where they were going," mused Rhonda. "We looked at their direction of travel and see nothing back there for a long way. At their current speed they wouldn't have gotten far even in all that time, and there's nothing out in front of them except intergalactic space."

"I'm quite sure they've been moved off the original course many times over the years," said Olga.

"Tell me again they have no weapons," said Jeannie.

"They have no weapons, nor do they have shields, at least none functioning that Probie could detect," said Linsey.

"Then I guess there's no real harm in letting you have a crack at it, Linsey."

"Jeannie ..."

"Yes, my conscience?"

Frank Baris chuckled at that. "We are going to help them if we can, aren't we?"

"Yes, Grandfather, if Linsey can manage to talk to them, we'll offer to help them if we can."

"That's good to hear," he grinned, "'cause, you know, pirates wouldn't do that sort of thing."

"Grandfather, you're not supposed to tease the admiral in a staff meeting. All right, Linsey, give it a shot. Sessas, you fly back up on this one, just in case."

Contact

Captain Linsey da Silva sighed and leaned back in her chair. Outside her small ship hung the slow moving monster ship, it remained unresponsive. She turned to her lover and constant companion, SUVI 18, the most intuitive of all the SUVI. "Eighteen honey, are you getting anything from that ship?"

"Far too much," came the soft reply. "I get fear, constant fear, anger, unrelenting hate, and more. Whatever is happening inside that ship, it isn't pretty."

"Do you need to go back to the Reacher?"

"No, I'm okay, but I would like to confer with Twenty on this, get her perspective."

"I'll invite her over," agreed Linsey. "Comms, get me the Retriever."

"Aye, Captain. Friendship calling Retriever, come in Retriever."

"Retriever."

"Captain Sessas, this is Linsey. Any chance Twenty could come for a visit to confer with Eighteen?"

"Will come now."

SUVI 20 arrived on the transport pad in a flash of light. "Hi guys, any luck?"

"Not a scrap," sighed Linsey.

"Twenty, you can guess what I'm picking up from that thing," said Eighteen. "What are you getting?"

"War," replied Twenty. "A long and bitter war. Two utterly opposed factions, each trying to wipe out the other."

"Okay, guys," said Linsey, "that's fine, but not helpful. What we need is a way to contact them. Do either of you think they know we're here?"

"They know," replied both SUVI in unison.

"Are they aware we're trying to make contact?"

Both women took a deep breath and let their eyes go slightly out of focus. Those eyes began to glow amber as they searched for an answer with all their enhanced senses. Eighteen just shook her head, but Twenty nodded. "I believe one faction may be aware and wanting to respond, but are unable to access the required tech, at least, that's the impression I'm getting."

"Can't access the tech?"

"Yeah, either it doesn't work anymore, or the other group holds the territory where it would be located. Just my guess, Linsey."

"What you say makes sense, Twenty. Tagora, could our transporter reach in there to bring someone out or to drop us in?"

The small Earalith woman smiled as she looked up and nodded. "Easily, Captain Linsey."

"Good to know. Comms, get me the Admiral."

"Aye, Captain Linsey. Friendship to Admiral Sorenson."

"Sorenson here. What's the good word, Linsey?"

"It's a bust, Admiral. Twenty came over to confer with Eighteen and they agree that there is a war going on over there. They believe one faction may be open to contact, but their opponents hold the tech stations."

"I know what you're thinking, Linsey, you want to transport over. Eighteen, don't let her do it, that's a job for a SUVI or the Strikers."

"The strikers could go as bodyguards," grinned Linsey.

"I don't like it, Linsey," replied Jeannie. "According to our sensors there's nothing over there we could use. We should just leave them alone and go on our way." There was a long pause, and they could hear voices behind Jeannie.

Finally she spoke again. "You humans will be the death of me yet. All right, Linsey, but you take the strikers with you, and you choose your landing site carefully. You go in wearing full armor and fully armed, understood?"

"Understood, Admiral." Grinning, Linsey turned to the woman on sensors. "Tagora, see if you can find me a small group that appears to be trying to access anything that looks like a control room.

As she spoke the Strikers from Retriever appeared in Friendship, armed to the teeth. "What are we facing, Twenty?"

"No idea, Billy. Linsey is going to drop us in near a small group, and she'll be with us. Our job is protection, her job is to make contact."

"Your job is to keep her safe no matter what she says," said Eighteen as she began pulling on her armor.

"Eighteen honey, I need you to stay with the ship."

"If you insist on going into danger, Linsey, I will be at your side to protect you, Ettelan can hold the ship. Tagora, stay at the transporter and the instant I signal, pull Linsey out of there."

"Aye, Captain Eighteen," chuckled the small woman, "moving to transport. Soran, you have sensors."

"Sensors, aye," smiled the second Earalith woman as she moved over.

Linsey just grinned and reached for the armor Eighteen passed to her.

* * * * *

"Get back, get back," shouted Tonts as he urged his companions back around a corner. The damned Growes had a full score of spearmen guarding the door of the control room. Somehow they had to get inside and figure out how to contact the outsiders, it was the only chance.

Their respite was short as the Growes rounded the corner intent on blood, and at the same instant, several outsiders appeared in the corridor.

To Linsey's utter horror, everyone attacked everyone else, and there was no way to tell them apart. Her mind had barely registered what was happening when she vanished to reappear back on her own ship. The rest of her team also began reappearing.

"Did we get everybody?" shouted Billy, leader of the strikers. "Rayla, where the hell's Rayla?"

"We got one comm badge without a person attached, Commander," said Tagora.

"She's alive," said Eighteen who had stepped to the sensors. "The landing area is clear, no life signs there and no dead bodies. Either she managed to escape or was taken captive."

"Gear up," barked Billy as he readied his weapon, "we're going back in."

"Not just yet, we need a better weapon for this."

"Twenty?"

"We need a SUVI hunter, Billy," said Twenty as she reached for her comm. "Twenty to Captain Sessas."

"Sessas, what wrong?"

"We lost Rayla but believe she's still alive. Suggest we go back in to retrieve her, but I'd like to have a SUVI hunter join us."

"Sessas agree, will check with Admiral. Sessas to Admiral." It took a moment then she got a reply.

"Sessas, what's happened?"

"Crew land on ship, all go crazy, pull crew out. Rayla not come back, still alive. Need SUVI hunter for retrieval mission."

"Agreed. Sorenson out. SUVI 5 calling SUVI 12."

"Here Five."

"We lost a striker on the alien ship, but she's still alive. They requested a SUVI hunter to join the retrieval mission."

"Which ship are they on?"

"Friendship."

"On my way."

A few short moments later a heavily armed SUVI 12 appeared on the transport pad of Friendship. "Twenty, what are we facing for weapons?"

"Blades, spears, no bows or other weapons. They're humanoid, fast, strong, and fight like animals, wild, uncontrolled."

"So, are we ready?" asked Linsey. "Let's get going."

"Hold on, you're not going anywhere," said Eighteen.

"I have to, Eighteen. This was all my fault, my dumbass idea; I lost her and It's my responsibility to get her back."

Eighteen stepped in front of the distraught woman and placed her hand firmly on Linsey's shoulders. "You're a diplomat, a language expert, not a hunter or a fighter. Remember Stormy. You work far better from the ship than in combat. You're staying here where you'll be safe, where you can be more help to the hunters."

"She's right," said Twenty. "You need to be here and Eighteen will stay with you."

"Twenty?"

"The admiral will have my hide if I take you into combat and you know it. Ready, people?" There was a round of agreement. "Send us over, Eighteen. Drop us where it went all to hell, and we'll work from there." They disappeared in a flash of light.

"She left you here because of me, didn't she?"

"No, my love," sighed Eighteen as she gently took Linsey in her arms, "she left me here for you. There's a big difference."

"What's the difference?"

"Right now you're upset and trying to take responsibility for what happened. Linsey, none of that was your fault."

"Yes it was, it was all my idea. I took an unnecessary risk, put everybody else at risk, and we lost someone. I'm responsible."

"Captain Linsey, if I may," put in Tagora. "Our mission is to learn new languages and to contact new people. You wanted to do your job, and the admiral agreed. The admiral and Captain Sessas formed a plan to keep you safe to do that job, but things went awry as they so often do when working with the unknown. What happen wasn't anyone's fault, Captain Linsey."

"She's right, my love," said Eighteen. "Not your fault, just the luck of the draw. Now, take a deep breath then figure out a way to find Rayla before the hunters do."

Linsey nodded and smiled sheepishly. "Okay, I guess you're right. Thanks guys. So she's lost her comm badge, that makes finding her a lot harder. Is there any way we can pick out her life sign from all the others?"

"No, sorry, Captain."

"Dang. Can we broadcast into that ship so everybody there can hear us?"

"I'll see if I can tap into their systems, Captain," chuckled Ettelan.

* * * * *

The strike force arrived on the ship in a group, the corridor was now empty. "Okay, so now what?" asked Billy.

"Now we let Twelve take over," replied Twenty. "Do your thing, Twelve."

Twelve nodded then began to study the immediate environment. There were no signs to read on the hard metal floors, but there was something. "Stay put for a minute." Testing the air for scent, she cautiously made her way along the wall.

Yes, it was there, very slight, but it was there, a human scent, quite different from the alien scent. She inhaled deeply several times until she was sure she had it. With a wave of her hand, she beckoned the others to follow her. "You say those creatures move fast?" she asked as Twenty reached her.

"Yeah, and apparently they're always on the move."

"Then she was captured but escaped them."

"Oh?"

"Their scent surrounded hers up to this point then they went that way, and she went this," replied Twelve as she moved off in a new direction.

"Company's coming," said Billy as he gazed at the instrument in his hand. He dropped it to the hook on his belt and swept his blaster to the ready. "Lots of them."

"Great," muttered Twelve, "and not a scrap of cover in sight."

"What's the plan?" asked Twenty.

"We use blasters to hold them off, and you and I capture a couple of them. You and the strikers take them back to Captain da Silva so she can get the language then maybe we can learn some useful things."

"What about you?"

"I'll stay here and continue the hunt."

"Twelve?"

"Twenty, my sister, I hunted alone on Elysium for years, and it was a damn sight more dangerous than this is, besides, now I've got much better weapons."

She was grinning wickedly and Twenty chuckled. "All right, if you're sure. Do you want to borrow the war maiden, you know, just in case?"

Twelve laughed at that. "You'd just beat me up if I got your pretty hammer scratched up. It'll be fine, Twenty. We know there are two factions over here, but no idea which one is coming. We might grab the wrong one for all we know. You take them back and I'll stay on the hunt."

Further conversation had to wait as a dozen or more strange creatures carrying crude weapons came from a different corridor and spotted them. They stopped, unsure of what to do. SUVI 20 spread her arms wide and stepped toward them. "Hi guys, I'm friendly. Any chances for a hug?"

Two of them leaped forward and grabbed her by the arms. That was a big mistake. She threw them back toward her people where Twelve grabbed them and the strikers opened fire with their blasters, hurling the others back and away. "Got 'em, Twelve?"

Both creatures were in restraints, both hand and foot, and whimpering in fear. "Got 'em, Twenty."

"Twenty to Friendship."

"Here, Twenty," came Eighteen's voice.

"We have two volunteers for Linsey to interrogate. Bring us back, but Twelve wants to stay here and continue the hunt alone."

"That figures," chuckled Eighteen. "Prepare to transport."

Twenty and her strikers disappeared with their captives. Twelve tested the air again then set out in a different direction. It was easier now without the other human scent close by. She bit down hard on the sudden empty spot inside her as SUVI Twenty left the ship. She would ignore that and hunt as she had so many times before.

* * * * *

Rayla Mills huddled behind some sort of mechanical projection, ever wary of approaching danger. "Well, girl, you're in the soup this time," she muttered to herself. "Let's see now, sprained ankle, but not broken, a few scratches on the armor, but no injuries to speak of. Damn, that bugger bit down hard, thank the gods for Jake's new armor.

"Okay, weapons, side arm gone, blaster gone, knife gone, baton still here. Okay, so it's the baton or nothing. What else is missing? Small med kit gone, rations gone, aw crap, the comm badge is gone and so is the universal translator.

"Right, so what's the next move? Well, Captain Sessas will send Billy and the strikers back to look for me, so I need to get back to the landing site as soon as I can. Okay ankle, hold me up now."

She struggled to her feet and tried to take a step, but the ankle wouldn't hold. Cursing madly, she sank back to the floor, fighting off the tears of fear and frustration. "Don't you dare, Rayla, don't you dare start crying. Billy wants to go back to Security, and you want his job. The Strikers are tough, they won't follow a crybaby. You stop this crap and plan your next move."

She wedged herself further back so no one could get at her easily. Still fighting back the tears, Rayla admitted to herself she was exhausted. The ankle needed time to heal, and she needed to rest. That had been a fight like none she'd ever faced before.

They'd landed in the corridor, but before anyone could move it went to hell as everyone attacked everyone in sight. Rayla had been tackled from the side and dragged away. She'd hurt three of them badly, but the numbers bore her down. She was aware as her people transported out, but she was left behind, her comm badge gone.

The creatures had dragged her along and she let them until she was sure they were relaxing a bit then she struck. They ripped and tore at her trying to penetrate the armor but all they managed to do was strip away her weapons and equipment. Her fists and feet took a terrible toll and they let her go to defend against another group that arrived. In the madness that followed, she'd slipped away.

Rayla succumbed to the fatigue and drifted off to sleep. She awakened screaming her battle cry as she was grabbed and hauled from her hiding place by her injured foot. She kicked off the one that gripped her leg then got to her feet and lashed out with the baton. One went down with a cracked skull and another with a broken arm.

The other two leaped at her, but they were tackled by a hurricane as SUVI 12 tore into them, battering them aside. The creatures fled leaving Rayla alone and sobbing in the arms of a SUVI. "Sorry, I'm sorry," she sniffed as, embarrassed, she pushed away from her rescuer.

"None of that, now," said a soft voice as gentle arms pulled her close again. "You've been in one hell of a battle, been hurt, and now face the adrenalin downer. You get back here and let me hold you."

"I'm okay, honest."

"You're not," replied Twelve as she gently pulled Rayla down onto her shoulder.

With a sniff and a sigh, Rayla melted against her rescuer. "Okay, but don't you dare ever tell anybody what a crybaby I am."

"Lips are sealed," chuckled Twelve. "Let me share a secret with you, we SUVI often did this for each other. Five has cried on that shoulder many times and she's held me while I completely came apart. This is a SUVI thing, so stay right there while I fish out some ration bars for you. The food will restore you, then we'll transport back to the ship."

"You're SUVI 12, aren't you? I'm Rayla. Why don't you want to go back now?"

"Because you're not ready yet. Eat the bar and catch your breath. When you're ready we'll go back."

"You're one of the hunters, aren't you? How did you find me?"

"Yes, I'm a hunter. It was discovered I could follow a scent when I was thirteen so First Prime made me a hunter. Here's two sharp knives, now off you go to the surface and bring back some meat."

"He sent you out alone with just knives?"

"Yes, always the SUVI hunted alone. We're herd creatures and don't like being alone. That way he knew we'd always come back to be with the rest of the SUVI. I followed your scent, saw the blood where you messed them up and escaped, then followed you here."

"Wow, that's a talent worth having. Twelve, thanks for coming for me."

"Feeling better now?"

"Yeah, I am ... oh shit."

"I felt them coming. How many?"

"Too many."

"Time to go home," said Twelve as she stuck her comm badge on Rayla's shoulder and hit the call button. "Got her, Eighteen, pull us out."

Before the transport could happen Twelve was tackled by a number of creatures and dragged away from Rayla who fearfully jumped back to disappear in a flash of light.

Hunting for a Hunter

The Strikers reappeared with their two captives. "What the ...?"

"Hi Linsey," grinned Twenty. 'We brought you a present. These two characters just volunteered to help you get the language."

"Okay, how is that supposed to work with their mouths taped shut?"

"Oh, right, sorry, my bad," replied Twenty as she ripped the tape away from the mouth of the female eliciting a yelp of protest. A similar protest was heard from her male companion as his tape was removed. Twenty picked up the female and carried her to a seat where Linsey could get her equipment close. She was surprisingly gentle as she brushed the creature's hair back from its face.

Linsey approached and sat facing the woman. She turned on her equipment then smiled and made eye contact with her. "Hi, I'm Linsey, what's your name?"

She got no response except a look of confusion, she tried again. Linsey patted her chest as she spoke her own name. "Linsey." She then held her hand toward the woman with a questioning look. She tried again and this time she got a response.

"Keta," the woman responded hesitantly, her voice rough and gravelly sounding.

Linsey lit up with delight. "Okay, we have a start, but now we need more. If you talk to me a lot the machine will be able to help me understand you. I know you can't understand me right now, I'm just demonstrating what I need you to do." She finished and held her hand out to the woman.

Puzzled, the woman just gazed fearfully at her, not knowing what was expected. "I can't understand you; I don't know what you want from me. Are you going to kill me?"

She was even more puzzled as Linsey lit up with a bright smile and made hand motions for her to keep talking. The strange box beside

Linsey made a few sounds that almost made sense. Suddenly the light of understanding reached her eyes. She began to jabber swiftly, talking directly to the box beside Linsey.

After a few moments the box began to repeat Linsey's words to the woman and a few of them she could understand. The Outsider needed her to keep talking until the box could understand and translate for them. She kept going.

Standing back watching, Twenty turned to Eighteen. "I don't get it; can't you just hook her up to Friendship and have her learn English?"

"Oh, yes we could, but then we'd need her to translate for the rest of her people. This way Linsey gets a new language for her database, and we'll have full access to the language."

"Gotcha. This way she can't pull a fast one on us later. I like it."

Just then Linsey gave a shriek of victory. "Yes, we've got it. Okay, hi there, I'm Linsey and you're Keta. We won't harm you Keta, be still now and we'll get those restraints off you." The box dutifully translated her words and Keta sighed with relief and relaxed. Twenty stepped forward and cut her bonds.

"Is the language in the database yet, Linsey?"

"Just another minute, Twenty." Her machine beeped and she grinned. "Try it now."

Twenty put on a bright smile and face the woman she'd tossed around so easily. "Hi, I'm Twenty. Happy to meet you, Keta. Can you understand me?"

"Yes, I can understand your words."

"Awesome," grinned Twenty as she turned away to the other captive. "All right you, I know you can understand me. I'm going to cut you loose now, don't make me regret it." He nodded that he understood. She cut his bonds and stood him on his feet. "Go sit down and behave."

He fearfully went to sit beside Keta. He had felt Twenty's strength before and didn't want to annoy her. "Okay, we've accomplished your mission, Captain da Silva, what's the next step for you?"

Before Linsey could the comms leaped to life. "Emergency transport now."

Tagora instantly flipped the switch and Rayla appeared on the transport pad, her wail of protest still on her lips. "Noooo, dammit, get me back in there."

Even as she spoke her injured ankle failed her and she fell sideways into Twenty's arms. "Rayla what happened?"

"Twelve found me, but we were attacked. She jammed her comm badge on my uniform and called for extraction, but they grabbed her before the transport got her. I need to get back in there and ..."

"Easy now, superwoman," grinned Twenty. "You need a medic; I'll go back for Twelve. Twenty calling Retriever."

"Sessas here."

"We've got our lost Striker, Captain, but she needs a medic. Twelve didn't make it out; I'm going back for her."

"Tentee, wait. Send Rayla home, wait for my call before go back."

"Aye, Captain Sessas, waiting." She winked at Tagora who sent Rayla back to Retriever.

The Retriever was not only a ship carrying striker troops to find and rescue explorers in need, but she also carried a full medical bay with three medics. Rayla soon had a shot to kill the pain and speed up the healing as well as a snug bandage. She struggled back into her boot and begged her captain to be sent back to assist Twenty in her search for SUVI 12.

"Sessas understand, Rayla. You go, be careful."

"Thank you, Captain." While Rayla stepped to the transport pad, Captain Sessas called the admiral and reported in.

Rayla reappeared in Friendship and was trying to convince Twenty to let her go on the rescue mission when the admiral contacted Twenty.

"Twenty, my sister, what are you up to now?"

"We had a small issue, Jeannie, and Twelve sent Rayla back by herself. Twelve's still over there, alone. I know all too well what that's like, and I had Jake to help me. I'm no hunter, but even if she has to find me it will be a lot easier on her with another SUVI on that ship with her."

"Wait for me, I'm on my way."

"Yes ma'am," she replied, but the comms were already off. A short time later the entire crew of the admiral's personal fighter ship was transported onto Friendship. Wide eyed, Twenty faced them. "Jeannie?"

"In the old days the SUVI had to hunt alone, they knew we'd always come back as SUVI need their herd. Those days are gone. A SUVI is lost on that ship, and the SUVI are going to get her back."

"And I'm going with you ... Admiral."

"Rayla, correct?"

"Yes Ma'am, I'm Rayla."

Jeannie gazed into the woman's eyes then nodded. "As you wish, you're Twenty's bodyguard. She's always getting into mischief so keep an eye on her. Twenty and I will take the Strikers, Nine, you take the crew and lead the hunt. We'll split up and stay in touch with the comms."

"Understood, Five. First SUVI team ready for transport." The crew of F1 vanished onto the alien ship then Suvi-jean, Twenty, and the Strikers stepped onto the platform to disappear in a flash of light.

The landing spot was already vacant as they appeared. "They didn't waste any time," chuckled Twenty.

"All right, my sister, which way?"

Twenty's eyes turned amber as she gazed around. "This way," she said as she led off, Rayla struggling to stay close on her left. If it went crazy, Twenty would use that Warhammer; she'd need room on her right.

* * * * *

Rayla was safely back on the ship as Twelve was swarmed by the creatures, clawing and biting at her trying to penetrate the armor. At that point something deep inside her cracked, perhaps it was the Orak's natural survival instinct. Whatever it was it gave her an adrenalin rush like she'd never had before.

With a wild scream of primal fury she fought back, no longer caring how many she killed or how much damage she inflicted. They soon fled from her in terror, five dead lay at her feet and eight more wounded trying to crawl away. Her eyes glowing nearly red, she broke free and fled in the opposite direction.

Twelve didn't go far before she reached a wide open area that stretched out as far as she could see. She stopped and gazed in wonder as the vista before her was utterly amazing. It was a jungle, sweeping out and curving up the vast walls. With a soft groan she sank to the floor to take in the view.

A sigh that was a near sob escaped her lips as she felt the aftereffects of the adrenalin rush, the depressing fatigue that could eat into your very soul claimed her and she groped for the high energy ration bars. Gone, the small pack had been torn away in the battle, as had her blaster and pistol.

"Ah well," she sighed, "I've hunted with knives before, might as well get to it." She struggled back to her feet, beating back the well of despair that tried to swallow her whole. "Crap, I hate adrenalin downers."

Suddenly her heart swelled with relief and hope, the SUVI had arrived, and she instantly felt their presence. With a warm smile on her lips SUVI 12 sank back to the floor to gaze at the spreading jungle before her while she waited for her rescuers.

She didn't have long to wait. A sound behind her made her smile. "You're losing your touch, Five."

"I never could sneak up on you, Twelve. Are you injured?"

"No, but I'm hungry. I was just about to go hunting when I felt you arrive on the ship. Got anything with you?"

"I do, here, you need this," said Rayla as she passed Twelve a high energy bar. "You made a hell of a mess of those guys who attacked us. Adrenalin downer?"

"Big one. Thanks," replied Twelve as she accepted the bar Rayla had opened and passed to her. "So, what the hell are you doing back here, I sent you for medical."

"I'm good, all fixed up."

"She threatened to shoot me if I didn't let her come back for you," grinned Twenty.

Rayla was blushing and Twelve was gazing at her with a puzzled expression. "What?"

"Thank you," replied Twelve. "I expected the SUVI to come, I guess it never occurred to me a human would volunteer to rescue me."

"We're not all bad guys, geez," grinned Rayla as she offered her hand to help Twelve to stand.

Twelve accepted the hand and rose easily to her feet. "Got any more of those energy bars?" Rayla passed her another then pinned a new comm badge on her uniform and activated it. "Thanks. So, Five, I can tell by the look on your face you're in no hurry to go home, you want to go hunting."

"This is amazing, Twelve. I've never seen anything like it," replied Jeannie, gazing in wonder at the jungle before her. "Yes, I'd love to go exploring this, so would you." Just then Nine and company arrived.

"Time to go, family. We've got company."

"How many?"

"A herd, Five. They remind me of Oraks. We should go."

"Agreed. Sorenson to Friendship, get us out of here." With a cry of dismay, Floo led his troops in a charge, but the outsiders vanished.

* * * * *

As soon as they all were back on Friendship, Jeannie spoke. "Linsey, take us home to the Reacher. Contact Sessas and ask her to join us."

"Aye, Admiral, gathering on the Reacher." She motioned to the man on comms who called for Retriever.

Jeannie called for Amanda. "Sorenson to Vice-Admiral Drake."

"Here, Jeannie."

"Call the captains and senior staff together with passenger reps. We've got things to discuss and Linsey's bringing friends."

"On it, Admiral," came that cheerful voice Jeannie loved so much.

What's Next?

"Floo, calm down, Floo."

"They escaped, Elee, they escaped."

Everyone else stayed well back out of Floo's reach, safer that way. Elee was the only one who could break through the madness that took him. "Floo, there is much to consider."

"Consider? Consider? The one we caught escaped, a new and different one came, and we caught them both, but the first one escaped. That new one fought us, killed many, and ruined several more. What more is there to consider?"

"They didn't feed, Floo. That strong one killed many but didn't feed on them. Why? Why would they not feed?"

Slowly he got himself under control. "You're right, she didn't feed on her kills, nor did she stalk and kill those who escaped. She also left the wounded there for us to find. Why?"

"Why indeed? Could it be they are not the ones of prophecy?"

"If not those then what are they? Why did they come and why did they fight us?"

"Think, Floo, how did this all start? What happened when we first saw them arrive?"

He sighed and looked away, his mind searching for the answer to her questions. "They appeared, the Gants saw them, we saw them, the Gants charged, we charged, the outsiders disappeared again, all but the one we captured.

"Obviously the strong one was sent to reclaim the one we caught, but for some reason wasn't able to escape with the first one. Bring me the things we gathered from them."

Several objects were brought to him. He rifled through the pack, finding several objects that he did not understand. He tossed each aside in turn then the empty pack followed. Next he inspected one of the other objects. As he poked and prodded at it the thing suddenly jumped in his hand with a loud bang. It tore the skin from his hand as he lost control of it, and another howled in pain as blood suddenly spurted from his shoulder.

Wide eyed with sudden fear, Floo hurled the object away. It clattered to the floor where it lay still and silent, foreboding. He stared at it for several moments before straightening up and reaching for the last object which vaguely resembled the last one. He poked and prodded at it for a few moments but didn't respond. He tossed it away too then it jumped and three of his men were sent tumbling over backwards.

As they picked themselves up Floo was staring at the object. "Floo?"

"Those are weapons, Elee."

"Yes they are, dangerous weapons."

"Why didn't the strong one use them against us?"

"I don't know, Floo. Could it be she didn't because we don't have similar weapons? Could it be that the outsider fought with tooth and claw as we do because it was honorable? Could these people be an honorable people?"

"Possibly, he admitted, "but they could also have been testing us, our strengths, and weaknesses. There's just no way to know.

"We must do things differently now. We know they're too strong to fight openly, and they have superior weapons. We must retreat into the forests. If they follow us there we must strike from hiding, before they have a chance to use those weapons on us. We've already lost too many fighters to them."

"But Floo," spoke up another, "if we do that the Gants will regain the room of control."

"I know, but there's no help for it. We can't hold the room of control from the outsiders anyway. We are beaten here; we must withdraw to the trees and hope to survive." They slowly followed him into the spreading jungle, carrying their wounded and dead with them. The Gants would find no meat left for them to forage.

* * * * *

"Sen Tonts," came a hesitant voice.

"What is it?"

"The others are gathered; they want to speak with you."

With a sigh, he rose and followed the woman to the outer room. All the Sens were gathered. He nodded and spoke. "Yes, it's true, Keta was taken by the outsiders; her fate is still unknown. With luck she will return with good news, for no greater ambassador could we have chosen to go to them. It also appears the Growes have withdrawn into the forests.

"The control room should be unguarded now. Shall we go see if we can make any headway now that we'll be left in peace to explore the possibilities?" There was a round of agreement, so he led them out and down the corridor to the room they'd so recently been driven away from. The Sens went inside, the rest stood guard.

* * * * *

"Looks like everyone's here, Admiral."

"Thank you, Vice-Admiral. All right, people, here's what we know at this point. There is an ailing ship beside us. We decided to offer them help to repair their ship and perhaps guide them in ways to improve it.

"With that in mind, Captain da Silva transported over to learn their language. The plan was to learn their language so we can talk to them. Unfortunately, as soon as she landed her party was attacked. They transported out immediately but lost one member.

"SUVI 12 led a rescue party to seek out our lost crew member. She was recovered, but in that process Twelve was lost. Also, SUVI 20 managed to find two volunteers from the aliens to board the Friendship and share their language with Linsey. They are here with us today.

"The SUVI successfully retrieved SUVI 12 and all is well on that front. So, now we learn a bit more about our new neighbors."

With that she stopped pacing and faced Keta and her companion. "We have the language now? You can understand my words?"

The small box on her uniform dutifully translated her words. "Yes," replied Keta, "I understand you."

"We mean you and your people no harm. Your ship is deteriorating and beginning to malfunction. We wish only to offer aid in the repairs."

"I understand."

"Why did your people not respond when we tried to contact you?"

"I don't know what you mean."

"What's your name?"

"Keta. I'm Keta."

"Keta, we have a way to project a voice over great distances. We sent our voice into your ship but got no response. Why did your people not attempt a response?"

"We heard no voice, Great Leader. We lost access to the room of controls, so we had no way to attempt a response even if we did hear the voice. The controls are ancient, and the means to use them have been lost through time.

"Tonts was trying to relearn their secrets, but the Growes drove us away from the last of the rooms of control that we had access to."

"Who are the Growes?"

"They are the Growes, the enemy."

"Why did they not try to reply to our call?"

"They would not know how; such things are beyond them. They only think of killing; besides they fear you bring the last death to them."

Jeannie sighed then went on. "So the Growes have no interest in technology. Explain what you mean by us bringing the last death to them."

"Long ago, Great Leader, in the golden time when Igen was brought into being by the ancestors, there came a prophecy. The peoples of Orra would face certain doom at the hands of outsiders. Igen was brought into being, and many people, both Gant and Growe, were placed inside. When Igen was ready she set out to escape the coming of the outsiders.

"In those times we Gants knew and understood the workings of Igen, but those days are long gone."

"What of the Growes? What was their purpose?"

"The Growes provided food, but it's difficult to acquire these days, and they drive us away from the rooms of control where we might regain some of the lost knowledge. You are the folk of the outside, the second prophecy says we can appeal to you for help."

"Second prophecy?"

"The prophecy is twofold, one says you are the destroyers, the other says you are the saviors. The Growes adhere to the old prophecy, but a few of the Gants lean toward the younger prophecy. That is why we wanted to regain the room of control, hoping to contact you and ask for help, help to repair Igen's ills, and to defeat the Growes."

"I am willing to consider helping with your repairs, but I will not involve my people in your war."

"Sadly, Great Leader, the one cannot be accomplished without the other."

"I find this idea disturbing." Jeannie turned and spoke directly to the man. "Tell me, are you in agreement with this? Do you also believe we must face conflict to help your people?"

The man looked up, confused. He turned to Keta who nodded. "Great Leader, I have no say in the matter, it is not my task to think of such things."

"What is your task?"

"To protect Sen Keta, nothing more. That is my task and my only task."

He grew uneasy as Jeannie gazed at him, a strange look on her face. "Tell me," she said gently, "is this a task you chose yourself, or was it chosen for you?"

"He is Ronton, what other purpose could he have?" asked Keta, confusion and fear on her face. She suddenly sensed great danger from the leader of the outsiders.

Jeannie's eyes had turned amber and her posture rigid. Fighting herself, she turned away. "Amanda, please take over here."

"Of course, Admiral."

Keta looked at this new person, a female of a slightly different species than the great leader, but obviously a person held in high regard by all. The woman approached and smiled. "Keta, tell me of your station among your people, the Gants?"

"Yes, we are the Gants. Tonts is our leader, and I'm his companion and his second."

"Just as I am second to my companion, the admiral. I understand. Tell me of the rooms of control, are there many, and if so, do you know which one was the main bridge, the room where the leaders of the Gants gathered in the early days of Igen's journey?"

Keta thought for a moment before she replied. "There is one, but it is deep in Growe territory, no living Gant has ever seen it."

"I see. That is most likely the one we need to access first. Tell me, if we send our voice into Igen now that we can speak your language, will the Growes listen to us? Will they stop fighting long enough to hear what we have to say? Will they listen to reason and allow us to repair Igen?"

"They may hear you, companion to the great leader, but they will not understand."

"They don't speak?"

"No, Sen Companion, they speak, but not as we do. You called it language, the language for the Growes is different."

"I understand. Thank you, Keta, you've been most helpful."

Amanda turned back to Jeannie whose eyes were still glowing amber. "It seems that we need a volunteer from these Growes to teach us their language if we're going to talk to them, Admiral. It also appears they control the main bridge, so we'll need that language if we going to access the bridge without bloodshed."

"Indeed so," replied Jeannie. "Hal, escort Keta and her companion to comfortable quarters. Keta, we will discuss this among ourselves then inform you of what we plan to do. You will not be harmed, nor will your ship."

"Thank you Great Leader, I anxiously await your decision." With that she turned to Hal who led her out of the room and signaled for a security officer to take them to quarters and stand guard. He then returned to the briefing room.

Inside Jeannie was pacing, her eyes still glowing amber. It was Captain Baris who broke the spell. "If I may, Admiral."

"Huh? Oh, sorry people. What was it, Grandfather?"

"Jeannie, our guest seems to have rubbed your fur the wrong way. What do you want to do here?"

With a sigh Suvi-jean returned to her chair and allowed her eyes to return to their normal green. "Good question. What I want now is your input, people. We've been informed that to help with repairs we'll need to go to war. Twenty, you were there. If we have to fight those people, what would we be facing?"

"Well, they're fast and strong. On an individual basis, they're easily a match for the Strikers. They're savage, use bladed weapons as well as tooth and claw. They can't penetrate our armor, but they fight in groups, swarm the opponent and try to strip away the armor."

"Your opinion?"

"We could defeat them easily using modern weapons and tactics. Admiral, I'd rather not have to do that."

"Me neither, my sister. All right, people, opinions? Options?"

"Well, if we try to contact these Growes with the language of their enemy, I doubt we'll get a hearing," chuckled Captain Moore.

"I can always use another language in the database," grinned Linsey. "Maybe this time we can just use our transporter to invite the volunteer aboard instead of risking our people."

"What happened there wasn't your fault, Linsey," said Jeannie, "but I do agree with your assessment."

"First you need to decide if we're going to get any further involved here, Admiral."

"Grandfather?"

"We could send our guests home and continue our journey. There is nothing aboard that ship that we need or can use. Do we have any right to interfere?"

"Good question. I do see your point, Grandfather. However, Keta did ask us for aid, and we did approach their ship with that intention. Do we now abandon them, or do we continue to offer assistance?"

"Don't be shy people, let's hear it."

"I'd like to investigate a bit further."

"Amanda?"

"I like Linsey's idea, get the second language and talk to those folks as well. Maybe we can broker a truce long enough to make their repairs for them."

"I like that idea," said Captain Volkov. "There's no harm in giving it a try, is there?"

"Are you all in favor of this?" There were nods of agreement all round. "I swear you humans will make me old before my time. All right, Vice-Admiral Drake, this one's your baby."

"Jeannie?"

"My darling Mandy, you saw how I reacted to that woman. We both know that man is her slave, and we know she has no idea of how she offended me. You have a much cooler head in this case. If I lead this one I'll probably sign the SUVI up with the Growes and fight the Gants.

"No, we wanderers need to remain neutral here, and I need to keep at arm's length from them. Just keep me up to speed on what you're doing."

"All right, Jeannie. I do agree, this is more of a social engagement task than a job for a warrior. Rhonda, we won't need the small ships for this, I'd prefer to work right from the Reacher."

"We're at your disposal, Vice-Admiral. What do you need?"

"Have your Chief of Security take Captain da Silva to transportation and find her a volunteer. Once she has the language in her database, I want to reconvene this meeting to see what we can learn then go from there."

"Yes, Ma'am. Hal."

"On it, Captain Moore," he grinned. "Captain da Silva, right this way."

As Hal led Linsey to the transportation area, Amanda adjourned the meeting.

* * * * *

While the top level meeting was going on, SUVI Twelve sat picking at her plate in the crew mess of Reacher. She was aware as someone approached her table and sighed; she wasn't really in the mood for company. She caught the scent and changed her mind, it was Rayla.

"Hi Rayla."

"How did you know it was me?"

"SUVI secret. What's on your mind?"

"You are."

"Me?"

"You. I like you and wanted your company, was thinking about you when I walked in and saw you there, lost in space."

"Lost in space?"

"Thinking about that magical forest in the other ship."

That made Twelve laugh. "Okay, you got me there, that's exactly what I was doing." Rayla grinned, she liked the sound of that laugh. "Did you need something, Rayla?"

"Just your company, like I said."

"What's going on?"

"A whole bunch of things, Twelve, plus I'm dying of curiosity."

"Curiosity? About what?"

"You, you and the SUVI. I really don't have a lot of contact with you guys, except for Twenty, and she's supposed to be way different from the rest of you."

"She is that," chuckled Twelve. "Okay, what do you want to know?"

"A bunch of stuff, and I want you to know something."

Twelve sighed. "All right, Rayla, I'll play along. Let's start right there, what do you want me to know?"

"I want you to know I understand. Understand how it must be for you, all of you. You're different, and there are only a few of you. I get how that is. I'm different from most people, always have been, and it gets lonely at times."

"You think I'm lonely?"

"Didn't say that, just saying I know how it can get sometimes."

"Okay, so let's move on to what you want to know. What's got you so curious?"

"Well, it's a couple of things, really. First, as I understand it, the SUVI don't like to be touched by a human, yet you held me when I melted down and ..."

"Hey, I left that part out of the report."

"I know," chuckled Rayla, "thanks for that. It's just that I didn't feel any hesitation from you then."

"There wasn't any. You needed it, and I remember having a few meltdowns after a hunt. It's okay, the secret is safe with me. What was the other thing you wanted to know?"

"Well, those guys came on us fast. I'm just curious, Twenty would have sensed them coming, but you didn't until they were almost on us."

Twelve sighed and looked away for a moment. "All right, I'll talk, but you keep this to yourself for the next eight hundred years."

"Okay, but after that I can blab, right?"

That elicited another of those wonderful laughs. "Yes, after that you can blab. All the SUVI are different. Eighteen and Twenty are scary intuitive, Thirteen can see possible futures, Three has the fastest reflexes of any of us, and more. I'm not intuitive, I function differently. My hearing is stronger, a lot stronger, and I can follow a scent as well as any animal.

"That's how I found you, I followed your scent. I didn't hear them sneaking up on us because I was distracted."

"Distracted? Oh, right. Twelve, can I make a confession?"

"Sure."

"I was pretty distracted at that point too."

"Rayla?"

"Okay, I'll confess, I like you and I really liked it when you held me. Nobody's ever done that before or wanted to. I liked it. I wouldn't mind doing it again sometime, if, you know, you wanted to."

Twelve sat staring at her. A full human, and she'd just confessed she'd enjoyed being held by a SUVI and wanted more. "Okay, we could do it again, I guess."

Rayla gave her a bright smile that seemed to light up her world. "Promise?"

"I promise."

"Then I'll call that a win and not push you any harder for now. We'll set up a time and place for that snuggle later." With that she rose and walked away.

"Oh, Rayla."

She stopped and looked over her shoulder. "Yes?"

"You don't have to get beat up first, we could skip right to the cuddle part."

Rayla shook a finger at her then walked away to the sound of that magic laugh behind her. She was grinning with delight.

A bemused Twelve went back to picking at the food on the plate, only now she was thinking about something other than the jungle on Igen.

Not Always Easy

Before Linsey managed to find her next volunteer, things went a bit crazy. "Captain Moore to Vice-Admiral Drake."

"Here, Rhonda."

"The Igen just went nuts, started using docking thrusters to change course."

"Change course, where are they going?"

"Circles by the look of it. They're slowing their spin as well, as I understand it, that spin is what creates their gravity. They could lose it soon and that'll create more interesting problems for them."

"They're messing with the controls. Okay, I'm on it. Drake out." She sighed then went on the comms again. "Amanda to Hal, have Keta and friend brought to me in Transport ASAP."

"Understood."

Amanda hurried to Transport and arrived shortly before Keta was herded in by two Security Officers. "Keta, I believe your people have gained access to Igen's controls, but they have no idea what they're doing. They've shut down the gravity generating system. This will cause untold damage to the ship and the people.

"I need you to go back and talk to them, convince them to let us come over to fix this while there's still time."

"Yes, I will speak to Tonts at once."

"Use this," said Amanda as she pinned a comm unit on Keta's tunic. "Touch it here to call me. Touch it again to end the conversation. Now, stand here and we'll send you home." She stood Keta and companion on the transport pad then nodded to the operator. Keta vanished from the Reacher.

"Where did you send them?"

"There was a lot of activity in the small room near where we first landed," said Linsey. "We sent them there."

"Well done, Linsey. Keep working on acquiring that second language, I'll be on the bridge watching the sensors."

"They still going in circles?" asked Amanda as she entered the bridge of the Reacher.

"Yes, they are," replied Captain Moore who was standing at the sensors with her second officer.

"Let's hope Keta can talk sense into them before they kill themselves."

* * * * *

"Tonts, Tonts, you must stop," shouted Keta as she appeared in the room with him and several others.

"Keta! Oh my beloved Keta," said Tonts as he wrapped his arms around her. "We feared you dead or worse."

"No, Tonts, I was taken aboard the outsider's ship and treated well. From me they learned to master our speech and they have offered to help us repair Igen. Oh Tonts, something you did in here has caused Igen to begin her death throes. You can feel her struggling beneath you.

"Tonts, the outsiders say they can help, they can heal Igen's hurts. Please let them. Please say you will let them come to help us."

"Of course I will, that's why we're here, trying to contact them."

"I will do that right now." She touched the button on her comm and spoke. "Vice-Admiral Drake, are you able to hear me?"

"I'm here, Keta."

"Tonts has given permission for your people to come, please help us."

"We'll send a repair crew over now. Ask all unnecessary people to leave that area so we'll have room to land. Drake out."

The comm fell silent and Tonts looked suspicious. "Keta, tell me you trust these people."

"I do, Tonts, especially that one. She is like me, companion to the true leader. That one I fear. I know not how, but for some reason I offended her. I felt her warmth withdraw from me to be replaced with a cold rage. She held herself in check and told her companion to deal with us, for she will not."

"This is distressing, but you still believe they will help us."

"Yes, but we must not try to harm or interfere with them, Tonts. They are powerful, and willing to help, but I fear if we annoy them we could cause the elder prophesy to gain prominence."

"Then we will be cautious when they are near. All right, everybody out, make room for the outsiders."

They withdrew from the room and looked back to see several outsiders appear in a flash of light.

* * * * *

"Ready Chief Engineer?"

"Ready."

Moira Duncan and two aides plus two heavily armed Security guards appeared in the small control room. "All right, lads, block the door, nobody comes in until I've had a look at the place." The two men nodded and stepped outside the door, effectively blocking entrance to the control room.

Moira and her engineers set to work with instruments, making notes of the readings, etc. "I'd say this one here controls the rate of spin that creates their gravity, Chief Engineer."

"Aye then, see if you can set it back to normal."

"From these readings I'd say it was slowly fading for a long time."

"Just take it back to where it was before we found them then see if you can stabilize it there."

"Aye, Chief. Working." A few moments later he spoke again. "Got it, stabilizing now." They felt the soft shudder then everything seemed to settle.

"That's good work, lad. Now, I can see a number of issues here. This is going to take a while, there's been no maintenance done in this ship in a long time. Okay, here's thruster control, just a minute now and ... there, that should do it. How's our course now?"

"Course is stable, Chief."

* * * * *

"Looks like they've stabilized the rotation, Vice-Admiral," said the second officer who was standing at the sensor panel. "Course has been corrected as well."

"Good to know. We've managed to do that much for them. Now we have to buy Moira enough time to figure out the workings of that old ship. This could take a while, and that means finding a means to create a truce with their enemies. I'll go see if Linsey is making any headway."

* * * * *

"Tonts, I can feel Igen sigh with relief. Feel the floor beneath us grow strong again?"

"I do. You were right, Keta. They will help us, but I wonder what they're doing in there now."

"Let's go ask them." She took his hand and tugged him toward the two Security guards that blocked the door. "Forgive us, great ones, but may we enter to ask questions?"

"Let her in, lads. As I understand it they're the leaders here," came Moira's voice. The two stepped aside to grant them entry then once again blocked the doorway.

"May we ask what you have done and what more you are doing?" said Keta.

"Come here," replied Moira. "See this pointer?" she asked as she tapped a glass covering that protected a dial and graph. "This must always point to this symbol here. This will keep the gravity stable. If it moves away it could cause disaster. Now, if it starts to move, use this lever to adjust until it returns to its proper position." Both Keta and Tonts nodded that they understood.

"Now, over here, these levers control a mechanism that can change the ship's direction to approach something or to avoid danger." Again they nodded. "As we learn more about the ship we'll show you what we've learned and what you can do to keep everything working smoothly."

"Thank you, great ones," said Tonts. "We will withdraw and let you work. We'll be right outside when you have more to teach us."

* * * * *

While Moira and crew worked to stabilize the ship, and Tonts eagerly waited for the chance to learn more, Floo paced beneath the broad-leafed trees. "Floo, what distresses you so? Igen has settled again."

"I know Eelee, and that tells me much."

"Such as?"

"The Gants have brought the outsiders into Igen. First, as we feared, the Gants began to meddle with things and disturbed Igen. The outsiders came and corrected the mistakes of the Gants."

"Is this not a good thing?"

"I fear the outsiders will teach the Gants how to control Igen. If that happens they will be able to gain full control of us again as well. We'll be returned to the pens as of old as the legends tell, easy prey for the Gants."

"So what will we do? We can't fight the outsiders, we know this."

"We still have the only access to the one room. Here beneath the leaves hides the room of full control, and we have it. We need to keep it hidden from the outsiders and the Gants. We must defend it to the death for it is our only hope of remaining free."

The others nodded their agreement and word quickly spread throughout Igen. The Growes began to gather in the sheltering forest.

* * * * *

"Wow," mused SUVI 18 as she gazed at the sensor panel in the main Transportation Room.

"What's going on, Eighteen?"

"Look, Linsey, all these life forms gathering in this area of the ship. See over here is where Chief Engineer Duncan and crew are working with the Gants, Keta's people. These gathering must be the Growes."

"Wow, I wonder what's going on? Think I'll call Amanda to have a look."

"Right behind you, Linsey," came Amanda's voice as she entered Transportation. "What's up?" Linsey showed her and explained.

"I think you're right, guys. I'll bet they're pulling back to defend a stronghold, and I'll bet it was the original bridge. Transport officer, grab two from those gathering there, any two at all. Security officers, stunners at the ready."

"I have a lock, Vice-Admiral."

"Bring 'em in."

The officer at the transport panel grinned as he threw the switch and two alien creatures appeared in a flash of light. They instantly leaped to the attack but were brought down by the stunners and lay on the floor twitching.

"Put them in restraints and make them comfortable while Linsey gets her equipment ready."

"Aye, Vice-Admiral." The two aliens were placed in restraints and chairs were produced for them.

Aloo awakened to find himself unable to move and sitting in a strange seat with a female outsider smiling at him. A glance to the side showed Selea starting to awaken. She was also bound to a chair. He brought his attention back to the outsider. She smiled again and spoke; he had no idea of what she'd just said.

"Hi there, welcome to the Reacher. My name is Captain Linsey da Silva. I know you can't understand me, but that's not the idea. The idea is to get you talking. So, what's your name?"

Aloo sighed and shook his head. "I have no idea what you said, Outsider. Just kill me now and I hope you choke on the meat."

She seemed delighted and motioned with her hand for him to speak more. "That's it, talk to me, talk to me."

"Selea, are you awake?"

"I am, Aloo. It seems we're done for. It is now our time to nourish, may they choke on the meat."

Suddenly the box the outsider held in her hand spoke a single word. "More." Both captives locked their eyes on the strange machine.

"Aloo, did that machine speak?"

"It did, just like the old ones said Igen used to do."

"Good, good, say more."

"Selea, I think that box is just changing her words so we can understand them."

"Yes, yes, it is," grinned Linsey. "Keep talking so the machine can better learn your way of speech. Soon we can talk to each other."

"Why not?" sighed Aloo. "Let me ask you this, do you enjoy tormenting your prey before you make the kill and feed?"

"I don't understand what you mean."

"You outsiders helped the Gants to regain the small room of control. They began to do things to Igen that should not be done. Obviously, you outsiders came to Igen and fixed the problem, but now you're teaching the Gants how to do this for themselves."

"Yes, that's what's happened. Now, the translator seems to have your language so let's start again. Hi, my name's Linsey, what's yours?"

"Why would you care what our names are? Stop this insane foolishness; just kill us and have done."

Linsey sighed and gazed at him. "Vice-Admiral, we have the language now, but I believe we have a cultural gap blocking progress here. Perhaps your training in social engagement is better suited to this conversation than my engineering background."

"I think you're right, Linsey," chuckled Amanda. "Hi there, I'm Vice-Admiral Drake, call me Amanda. First let me assure you, you will not be killed. We only want to talk, to exchange information and ideas, to offer our help to your people. So, what's your name?"

"Aloo, I'm Aloo, and this is Selea. You truly aren't going to kill us?"

"No, we just want to talk. We brought you here so Captain da Silva, Linsey, could help us learn how to talk to each other. Will you speak with us, or do you want to be put back where we found you?"

"Put us back."

"No, Aloo, no, let's talk to her. There is much we can learn here."

"You mean there is much they can learn that will help them put us back in the pens."

"I don't think so, Aloo. They are so powerful, they snatched us from Igen so easily, and we could not fight them. Think about it, if they want us dead they will make it happen. They snatched us from Igen, where could we ever hide from such people. She says they won't kill us; I believe her."

Slowly, he nodded his head resignedly and she turned her attention back to Amanda. "I'm Selea, we will speak with you. What do you want from us?"

"We want to learn about you, and for you to learn something about us. You can remove the restraints now guys."

The Security men removed the restraints then stepped back, watching the aliens carefully. Aloo rubbed the circulation back into his arms and smiled. "Thank you for that. What would you like to know, or for us to know?"

"We're here to help," replied Amanda. "Your ship, Igen, is in trouble, needs repairs. We are willing to help with those repairs, and we want to. However, there is a small problem. We had two visitors from Igen and they spoke of a conflict."

"Gants. Did they visit the same way we did?"

Amanda grinned at that. "Yes, there were two volunteers. Her name was Keta, and I have no idea what her companion's name was. She told us the Gants and the Growes are at war."

"We are," replied Aloo. "Floo realized what had happened and sent out the call. All Growes return to beneath the leaves where we can more easily ..."

"Defend the bridge?"

"Bridge?"

"The room where all controls for Igen can be found," smiled Amanda.

"Yes, defend the bridge," sighed Selea. "The Gants must never gain access to it. If all else fails, Floo will destroy it."

"No, he mustn't try to do that," said Linsey. "That could cause Igen to fail completely killing everyone."

"He knows," said Selea. "We all know and agree, if we are to die, better to take the Gants with us into the mystery than to be herded together and slaughtered one or two at a time."

"There is much I don't understand here," said Amanda. "Let's go slowly now so I can learn. Tell me of life on Igen. What is a normal day like for you? What things do you enjoy doing?"

Selea smiled wistfully. "We begin as the day lightens. If things are quiet, we eat some veg, then check the supplies, tend the trees, and see to the young. If we're assigned to hunt, then we set about the hunt. If we're assigned to guard, or tending wounded, then we do that. If it is a rest day then we often wander beneath the leaves, or even fall asleep deep in the forest."

Amanda nodded. "You say you hunt, what do you hunt?"

"Gants mostly. We hunt other creatures for meat, but mostly we hunt Gants."

"Why do you hunt the Gants?"

"To kill them. If we catch a smaller party we might get lucky enough to make a kill."

Amanda furrowed her brow as she carefully processed what she'd heard. SUVI 13 had taught her a way of processing he called critical thinking. Use your brain he'd often told her. She was working it now. "Okay, tell me why you want to kill Gants."

It was Aloo's turn to look perplexed. "So they can't kill us, may they choke on the meat."

"What does that mean, to choke on the meat?" asked Linsey.

Aloo looked totally bewildered, but the light of understanding reached Selea's eyes. She patted his arm and spoke. "They don't know us or the ways of Igen, Aloo. Let me. Amanda, Linsey, when the Gants kill a Growe, they eat the body and grow strong. Every Growe learns this from childhood, and we all hope that, if we're caught and killed, that our body will cause the Gants to choke on the meat and die."

"Eat the body?" exclaimed Linsey. "You're cannibals?"

"What is cannibal?"

"Cannibals are people who eat the bodies of their own species," said Amanda. "The idea is abhorrent to us."

"No, we don't eat our own," said Aloo, "nor do we eat the Gants we kill. We leave the bodies for them to eat, may they choke on their own meat. No, we Growes eat mostly of the veg that Igen provides and the meat that we can hunt beneath the leaves."

Amanda was thoughtful for a while and they didn't disturb her. Finally she returned her attention to their guests. "I confess our ways are closer to the ways of the Growes, but not entirely, but we do sometimes eat the meat of other species if we encounter something likely on a planet somewhere. Rest easy, my friends, we do not eat the meat of a sentient species.

"However, our ways are not your ways, and your ways aren't ours, and that's as it should be. It's not our intention to interfere in the way your people spend their lives. Our intention and purpose here is to learn about you and to help you repair Igen. We would also like to teach you how to better control Igen so she will last longer and give you safer lives.

"It would be a big help to us if we could access that bridge. Linsey could learn much from the old logs if such exist."

"What are logs?" asked Aloo.

"The logs are recordings of events," replied Amanda. "Each Captain of a ship records the events of the day so those who follow in time will know what happened and what was done about it. For example, Linsey is captain of a small ship. When she's on her ship she will record the events the ship encounters, and how she directed the crew to deal with that.

"When Igen first set out it is likely they had a similar system in place. Linsey could learn much from Igen's logs and she would share that knowledge with you, and through this your people would learn how to care for Igen."

"You would teach us the things you're teaching the Gants?"

"Yes."

"Selea, we must tell Floo of this. It will be for him to decide what to do."

"Floo, is he your leader?"

"Yes, all Growes obey Floo. Floo has led us for a long time, and many young Growes survived because of this. We have grown many and strong under his leadership."

Amanda nodded. "I will ask a favor of you both. Will you speak to this Floo for me, tell him we only wish to repair Igen and to learn about her people. We will teach you what we can about how to care for Igen then we will leave you to your journey. Will you do this for me?"

"Yes, of course," replied Selea.

"Then you will need this," smiled Linsey as she pinned a comm unit to Selea's tunic. "Touch this button here and say, 'Selea calling Amanda, or Selea calling Linsey.' One of us will respond to you. When the conversation is finished touch the button again to end the call. Try it now."

With wide eyes, she touched the button. "Selea calling Amanda." To her great delight her voice sounded from Amanda's shoulder then the box translated her words. Amanda smiled and touched the button on her shoulder. The box spoke so Selea could understand.

"Here, Selea, it's working perfectly. We'll send you both home now. Tell Floo we'd be happy to speak with him."

With that Amanda nodded to the officer at the transportation panel. Aloo and Selea disappeared to reappear back on Igen. There was a great deal of fuss and chatter at their surprise return and eventually they were brought to Floo and Eelee.

Making Plans

While Aloo and Selea were trying to get an audience with Floo and to convince him to let the outsiders have access to Igen's bridge, Amanda reported to Jeannie who called a meeting of Captains and Reacher's senior staff.

"Everybody's here, Admiral."

"Thank you, Vice-Admiral. People, we have more information from Igen and it disturbs me. Amanda, my delight, please share your report with everyone."

"Of course," smiled Amanda. "Okay folks, Linsey managed to find two volunteers from the Growes faction to talk to. While Chief Engineer Duncan and company were making a few repairs and course corrections on Igen and teaching the Gants how not to destroy the ship, we were conferring with the other side.

"As we had already learned from Keta, the Gants and Growes are at war. What we learned from the Growes is the reason why. Also, the Growes control the territory that holds the Bridge of that ship. Since we admitted we were teaching the Gants to use some of Igen's controls, we were informed the Growes would destroy the bridge and the ship with it."

"That's madness," exclaimed Moira Duncan.

"That's typical zealot thinking," sighed Captain Baris.

"Actually," said Amanda, "that's the result of the war and what started it. The Growes have a saying, and you will hear it often if you speak with them. May they choke on the meat, that's what they say. Apparently, the Gants hunt the Growes for meat. The Growes hunt the Gants for revenge."

That brought a hush over the gathering. Amanda sighed and went on. "I'm sure there is a lot more history behind this, nothing is ever that cut and dried. However, it does explain why the Growes would rather sabotage the ship and die as a group rather than be put in holding pens to be killed one at a time for food.

"I did say that we would teach them the same things we teach the Gants and that caused a bit of excitement, perhaps hope is a better word. We sent Linsey's two volunteers back to Igen to confer with their leaders. I'm hoping they'll agree to accept us, for that will give us access to the main bridge."

"Aye," agreed Moira, "that would make things a lot easier for certain."

"And we can learn so much more from the captain's logs if they survive," said Linsey.

"So, what's the next step?" asked Captain Baris.

"We offered these people help to repair their ship," said Jeannie. "The purpose in doing that was to help them remain alive and continue, even as we strive to do the same. However, it's becoming clearer that we must broker a peace between them, first to ensure the safety of our own people as they work, but also to help them understand they need to work together to survive."

"Good luck with that," chuckled Olga Volkov. "It was pretty clear when the Gant was here that they keep slaves, at least slave fighters, and now you say they're cannibals? That's going to be a tough one."

"Olga's right there," sighed Jeannie. "What's your next step, Mandy?"

"Well, first I want to talk to the leader of the Growes, get us entry to the bridge. Once that's accomplished, I want Linsey to go through everything she can find about the history of these people, see if she can unravel some of this and how it came to be.

"I doubt the Gants were cannibals when the ship first set out. I'm hoping that by understanding how all that came to pass we might get a few ideas how to unravel it and get them working together. If they're going to survive on that old ship they all need to cooperate and learn how to maintain it."

"That's the truth," said Moira. "As they are now this generation could be their last."

"Yeah, I thought so too," said Amanda. "Okay folks, I'm wide open to suggestions here."

"Go away, not come back."

"Sessas?"

"These folk like Sessas people, small group, too long alone. Not want change, want Reacher folk fix ship then go away."

"Sadly, Mandy, Sessas could be right."

"Maybe, but I'm not ready to quit yet. Sessas, your folk had a planet to survive on. Over time they could grow stronger, learn new things, become a different people. These people don't have that option. I want to help them if I can, but I need your help to do that. Will you help me?"

"Sessas help. What do?"

"Keep your strikers ready. If I get the chance I'm taking Morthel's explorers over there, we may need you to get us back."

"Mandy, what are you up to?"

"Jeannie, I'm betting the reason the Gants turned to cannibalism is they were the elite class, had no idea how to get their food, just like Jake on Stormy. The slaves probably rebelled and cut off the food supply. I'll need Lilly Peters to gather samples then devise ways for the most nutritious food source to be enhanced."

"Then you'll have to convince them to share that with the entire population," said Captain Baris. "I don't like it, not one bit of it. We're getting way off course here. The idea was to help them repair the ship and learn how to maintain it, not change their entire society."

Amanda turned her attention to the old captain. "Captain Baris, the idea is to help them repair and maintain the ship, as you say. Let me ask you why? Why would we do that?"

"To help them survive," he replied, somewhat perplexed.

"Agreed, sir, but even if we repair the ship they cannot survive as they are. If they're to survive, they must cooperate. I thought it would be easier to find the Gants another food source than to convince the Growes to make regular sacrifices."

Captain Baris chuckled at that and shook his head. "Amanda, you're starting to think like a SUVI. You have a good point there. I wish you luck convincing them to work together."

* * * * *

While their leaders were trying to sort out the bigger problems, Rayla Mills was trying to sort out an issue of her own. She entered the quarters she shared with her brother and plopped down in a chair.

"Oh my," chuckled her brother Kimmon, "someone's messed up."

"Shut up."

"I love it when I'm right. Okay, tell brother Kim what you've done." He passed her a container of water then sat facing her.

Rayla took a long sip from the water then sighed. "I made a complete fool of myself, and maybe worse." He didn't respond so she went on. "On that ship I got momentarily captured by the enemy. I fought them and got loose, but my comm was lost so they sent a SUVI hunter to bring me out. I've told you all this already.

"What I didn't tell you is I had a major meltdown while on that ship, in the arms of a SUVI."

"Uh-oh."

"Yeah, uh-oh. I had it under control then she put her arms around me and I melted down. I mean, you're not supposed to touch them, right, they don't like it. So what the hell ever possessed her to do that."

"Who knows," he chuckled, "but that's not the issue, is it? The issue here is how much you liked it."

That brought another huge sigh from her. "Yeah, that's the issue all right."

"And that's where you embarrassed yourself?"

"Yes and no. Yes, I cried on her shoulder, and she let me, held me until they found us. She sent me back alone and stayed to fight them. I joined the rescue party and we got her back."

"And that's when you ..."

"Yes indeed. That's when I went full Mills and stepped in it. I saw her sitting alone in the mess, went over and confessed how much I liked being held by her and asked if she would do it again sometime."

"Oh my, I'll bet your brain was trying to stop your lips."

"It was, but as usual, I ran my mouth before I could shut myself up."

"So what happened? What did she say?"

"She said yes, but I don't have to get all beat up first."

"Rayla, oh my god, you lucked out?"

"Yeah, I think I did."

"Okay, and the problem is?"

"You know me, Kim, I'm scared shitless I'll bugger this up."

"Aw, you won't mess it up, big sister," he said as he crossed over to sit beside her and put his arms around her shoulders. "You'll be just fine. It feels weird, doesn't it?"

"Huh?"

"Falling in love, it feels weird, scary and thrilling at the same time. So who is it?"

"What?"

"Your SUVI hunter, which one is it?"

"Twelve. What? What's that look for? What do you know about Twelve?"

Kim sighed and let his arms fall away as he leaned back in the seat. "Apparently she's as close to a loner as you'll ever find among the SUVI, a lot like you. Nobody knows much, and she doesn't talk to many people. She's assigned to EX4 as a gunner, likes the job, keeps to herself for the most part. She's a lot like you, really."

"Now I'm really scared I'll mess it up."

He pulled her back onto his shoulder. "Hush now, big sister. That's the over-tired talking now. Get some rest then we'll plan how to best lead SUVI 12 astray."

* * * * *

Twelve sat in her gunner's turret, fingers idly playing across the controls as her mind wandered. She sighed as she recognized the scent before she heard the voice. "Twelve, the ship is in the Reacher's landing bay. If you blow a hole in the hull the captain will not be pleased."

She chuckled at that. "Ebony, what are you doing here, is the ship launching?"

"Nope, I just came to see if I could find my ... ah, there it is," she said as she slipped an info stick into her pocket. "I need this for the next VR Edran is working on. So, anything I can do to help?"

"What???

"You're all messed up, hanging out in an empty ship, playing with the weapons controls. That tells me you've got something heavy on your mind."

"It's none of your damn business, human."

Ebony laughed and slid into the seat beside her. "Oh good, SUVI secrets, tell me all."

Twelve just shook her head and chuckled. "What's wrong with you, Ebony, I insult you and you act like we're best friends."

"We are, at least we're Cavern sisters of a fashion. No, I wasn't a slave, or abused like you were, I just hid in quarters, scared for my life every minute of every day. That gives me a tiny window into what you face every day now. It's confusing as hell some days and we're always overcompensating; afraid we'll mess up somehow."

Twelve gazed into her eyes for a long moment then looked away. "Yeah, that pretty well covers it."

"So, who is she?"

"What???"

"Oh come on, it has to be a woman, nothing else could throw a SUVI hunter off their game so easily. Look at poor old Thirteen, Connie almost has him domesticated."

Twelve howled with laughter at that. "Okay, you got me, it's a woman."

"So you found a girl and she lights your fire, now you're messed up because you don't know what to do next."

"Right on the money, so any idea what I should do? Come on, you're human and you've got a girlfriend. What's my move?"

"Relax and enjoy it, my friend," grinned Ebony as she rose and stepped out of the turret. The stricken look on Twelve's face melted her. "Okay, tell me."

"It's Rayla, the striker from Retriever. She got captured and I went in to bring her out. She approached me in the mess later and said she enjoyed my company and wanted more of it."

"And you said yes, and now you're scared, confused, and hiding out."

"Yeah, that. So, what do I do?"

Ebony sighed and sat beside her again. "Watch for opportunities to spend time with her, talk to her, enjoy her. Don't try to force it, let it evolve on its own. If it's good between you see where it goes."

"Just follow the trail and see where it leads?"

Ebony gave her a bright smile. "Yeah, that. I hope it works out for you, Twelve."

With that she rose to leave but turned back at the sound of Twelve's voice. "Ebony, thanks. Please keep this all to yourself."

"I will. Enjoy the hunt." She smiled and walked down the ramp.

"The hunt," mused Twelve. "Maybe that is the best way to do this, just follow the trail and see where it leads."

A Meeting with Floo

Floo turned at the sounds of the loud discussion nearby. "What's going on?"

"It's Selea and Aloo. They say they were on the outsider's world. They have news and a message for you from the outsiders."

"Bring them here."

Eelee nodded and hurried away but soon returned with the two missing people. "So, you claim to have been on the outsider's world, do you? I think you just sneaked off for a tryst under the leaves."

Aloo chuckled at that. "No, my brother, as much as the idea appeals, that wasn't what happened. They took us to their world in the same manner they came to ours, a sudden flash of light. One moment we were in Igen and the next in a very strange place. We tried to react, but they used their weapons and we were captured."

"But they let you go?"

"They don't eat the meat of sentient species, so they say. They just wanted to talk, to explain why they're here."

"They talk? You can understand their talk?"

Selea shook her head and sighed. "It was all so frightening, Floo. We were tied and one of them was smiling at us, making strange noises. It got excited when we told it to stop fooling around and just kill us, get it over with. It wanted us to keep talking. A few moments later a strange box began to talk back to us. The box learns our talk then tells them what we said, then tells us what they said in return. In this way we were able to speak with them."

Floo nodded. "I wonder, did we of Igen have such magic things in the bygone times? Ah well, did they say what they wanted? What was the message they sent you to bring to me?"

"They know Igen is failing. They admitted they helped the Gants and taught them some of the workings of Igen."

"I knew it," shouted Floo. "Tell me you saw a weakness, some way we can kill them before they put us in the pens again."

"No, Floo, we saw no such weakness. Floo, they don't want to put us in the pens, they don't want us for food, they only want to help us learn how to help Igen grow strong again. The message was to tell you they will teach the Growes all the things they teach the Gants. Floo, they want to talk to you."

"Why? What do they want?"

"The one room of control," sighed Aloo. "They called it the bridge. They promised to teach us how to understand and work the controls found there. They also said they can learn things about us there."

"Things? What kind of things?"

"How we became food for the Gants," replied Selea. "That and more. They say they can learn where we once came from and where the ancestors wanted us to go. Floo, you always say knowledge is power. This could be a chance to gain much knowledge."

"Yes, or it could be some sort of trap. I must think on this. How will we give them an answer, will they take you through the light again?"

"No, Floo, with this," smiled Selea. "Through the magic of this I can talk to them."

"Show me."

She nodded then touched the button as Amanda had taught her. "Selea to Amanda." Nothing happened so she tried again. This time she got a response.

"Amanda here, Selea."

"Amanda, Floo wishes to speak with you, will you hear him."

"Tell him to step close to you and I'll be able to hear him."

"Outsider, this one tells me you want to have access to the room of all control. She says you are friends, but the prophecy says you are destroyers. How can I trust your words?"

Amanda chuckled at that. "I'll show you mine if you show me yours."

"I don't understand."

"I'll show you the bridge on my ship first, then you show me the bridge on yours."

"You would take me into your world and show me the room of full control?"

"Yes, and then you show me yours. Is it a deal?"

"I will think on this and then decide."

"As you wish. Selea can contact me when you're ready. Amanda out."

"Out? What does that mean?"

"It means she's gone, Floo. She's letting you decide what you want to do. I'll call her again when you've made up your mind about this."

"That one was the leader of the outsiders?"

"No, her companion. The leader will not speak with us. The Gants visited them first and managed to offend the supreme leader of their peoples. The leader appointed Amanda to talk to the peoples of Igen. Amanda is powerful, the second in command, and yet, she is friendly to us. I trust her, Floo."

"Yes, well, I don't, not yet, however, her suggestion is intriguing."

"Floo?" Eelee looked surprised.

"Think about it, Eelee. Imagine what we could learn from visiting their room of control. How much could we learn there that would help us understand the controls of Igen?"

"So you're going to visit them?"

"It's worth the risk, Eelee. First we'll wait until the light fades then returns to Igen before we call them back. We don't want to appear too eager."

* * * * *

Amanda sighed and relaxed back in the bed. Selea's call had dragged her from a deep sleep. Jeannie cuddled her closer. "You offered to show him the bridge of Reacher?"

"A sign of good faith, sweetheart. The plan is to show him a bunch of things he doesn't understand but would love to learn. When we return him to his ship unharmed and with a thirst for more knowledge, he should be more than ready to give us access to his bridge. At least, that's the plan."

"I like it, Mandy. I'll send Thirteen with you."

"Don't you want to come?"

"I gave you this mission, sweet woman. I will not watch over your shoulder while you do it." Amanda chuckled at that and snuggled deeper into her embrace then went back to sleep.

* * * * *

While Amanda drifted back to sleep in the arms of her lover, Rayla sat in the mess, sipping at a cold tea and gazing blankly into space. Suddenly someone sat across from her, startling her from her reverie. It was Twelve. "Can't sleep?"

Rayla sighed and pushed away the half empty cup of Earalithian tea. "No, you?"

"My shift on EX4 just finished. Nightmare?"

"Good guess."

"It was a natural."

"Oh? What do you mean?" asked Rayla.

"I used to get them after every hunt. Elysium is a dangerous place and First Prime loved garog meat. If I could get one I could earn extra time with another SUVI, but it was a dangerous game. I had a lot of really close calls."

"And you had to hunt them with just knives. Gods, that was so wrong."

"We all made spears and hid them, so we'd have them when we needed to hunt."

"Smart," chuckled Raya. "What did you mean, extra time with another SUVI?"

"We SUVI are all connected to each other somehow. We don't do well alone. If we had a successful hunt we would be allowed to spend time with other SUVI. If Prime wasn't happy with the meat we'd be put into solitary for a week, or worse."

"Worse?"

"We'd spend time with him."

"Oh gods, Twelve, I'm so sorry. I should have known better, should have kept my mouth shut. I ..."

She stopped as Twelve reached over to take her hands and squeeze them gently. "Easy, Rayla, easy. It's all right. Look, I get the sense you want us to spend time together, I think I'd like that, but I'm SUVI. We're different, there are things about us you need to know, and a lot of it has to do with the way we lived on Elysium."

Rayla gazed into those deep brown eyes for a long moment, keenly aware that Twelve was still holding her hands. "Teach me, teach me what I need to know. I ...I don't want to hurt or offend you; I want you to like me." With that she blushed furiously and lowered her gaze to their entwined fingers.

"Wish granted," smiled Twelve. "I do like you, Rayla. You're more like a SUVI than you know. Okay, teach you. Sure, but I'm probably not the best for this. You learn to hunt by hunting."

"What? Oh, you mean I learn about the SUVI by spending time with you and pestering you with questions, right?"

Twelve chuckled and released her hands. "Right. So, we begin with this. My instinctive accuracy with weapons was a big part of my success as a hunter, that's also why Five wanted me on EX4 as a gunner."

"Okay, so now I know you track by scent as well as by sight and you're a deadly shot."

"That's a start, but you know more. To follow a trail successfully, you need to see everything in the environment and understand its meaning, its relationship to the quarry and what it might mean for your eventual success. As Thirteen says ..."

"Use my brain, yeah, I've heard about that one. Okay, what I know about the SUVI, no, wait, only one SUVI is the object of my interest here. The real question is, what do I know about SUVI 12. Okay, she hunts by scent and sight, is a crack shot, and a super hugger. What else?

"She's a bit of a loner like me, but as a SUVI, she truly needs to be with other SUVI, so if I'm trying to track her down that's a good place to start." That brought a laugh of delight from Twelve.

"What else do I know about Twelve? She's a fierce and deadly warrior, a natural survivor, but yet she sent me to safety and remained behind to face the danger alone. Why? That's not a natural prey instinct unless ..." Rayla's eyes opened wide as realization of what had actually happened on Igen hit her.

Twelve nodded and gave her a shy smile. "Keep going."

"Unless she was protecting a mate or offspring, someone special. Twelve?"

"You're a pretty good hugger yourself."

This time Rayla reached to grasp Twelve by the hands. "Talk to me, Twelve. Help me to understand."

Twelve looked at their joined hands for a long moment before she spoke. Finally she looked up to gaze into Rayla's eyes. "I discovered another SUVI instinct on that damned ship, a part of me I didn't know was there. As I said before, the others are more intuitive than I am, so this caught me by surprise. When I held you it was instinctive, I needed it more than you did, I needed it from you. Something inside me said this woman is precious beyond all else.

"Sorry, I'm not explaining it very well."

"Me being a puss, a crybaby, triggered your mating instinct?"

Twelve shook with laughter at that. "Yes, that. Shocked the hell out of me, but all I could think of was to get you out of there to safety. That and look for a chance to steal another hug."

Rayla sighed and squeezed the hands in hers. "No one has ever called me precious before. Gotta admit, I like the sound of it. I'll confess, when you held me I felt truly safe for the first time I can remember, and I wanted more, lots more."

"Yeah, I wanted more too. Those blasted Growes showed up and ruined the whole thing, damn their hides. So, my precious girl, we have now entered the territory where I have no experience at all and absolutely no idea of what to do next. It's obvious we both want a bit more than a just a cuddle session once in a while."

"I'm as lost as you are, Twelve. I've never been in a relationship before, and I have no idea what the heck we do next."

"A relationship, is that what this is? Is that what you want?"

Rayla sighed and squeezed those fingers again. "Yes it is. If you don't then ..."

"Stop now. I want that too; I just don't know how it works."

"Me neither. Shall we figure it out together as we go along?"

"Fine by me. Now, you're falling asleep on me here, how about I walk you back to your quarters and you get some rest." Twelve rose and gently pulled Rayla to her feet.

They walked along together, still holding hands, until they reached Rayla's quarters. With a deep sigh of fatigue, she turned and stepped into Twelves arms, hugging her tightly. "Get some sleep, my precious girl," whispered Twelve as she returned the hug enthusiastically.

"You need rest too, my super SUVI," said Rayla as she reluctantly stepped out of Twelve's embrace and reached for the door. The door slid open and her brother stepped through, bumping into both of them.

Rayla caught Twelve's hand as it streaked for Kimmon's throat. "No, honey, this is my brother Kim, the only other person who ever gave a damn if I lived or died."

Twelve relaxed her arm and patted his shoulder. "We need to talk."

"We do?" asked Kim, wide eyed.

"Our Rayla needs to rest, but we need to talk. You know much of what I need to know to make her life better."

"Oh no," chuckled Rayla as she saw the teasing twinkle in Twelve's eye. "You're not getting all my secrets out of him before I have a chance to figure you out. Kim, get to work or you'll be late. Twelve, go home and get some sleep."

"Yes ma'am," grinned Kim as he hurried away.

Smiling, Twelve gave her another gentle hug then walked away. Rayla watched her go then went inside and shut the door. On the way to her bedroom she did a twirling little dance of glee where no one could see her do it.

While Rayla got some much needed rest, Amanda rose and prepared for her day, hoping to hear back from the Growes. She had a long wait.

The Visit

Floo eventually agreed to Amanda's request and he, accompanied by Selea and Eelee, arrived to be met by Amanda. She was flanked by Twelve and Thirteen with the rest of EX4's crew standing close by. "Amanda, this one is our leader, Floo, and his companion, Eelee," said Selea. "Floo, this woman is Amanda, companion to the leader of the outsiders."

"I greet you, Amanda," said Floo. "I see you have several Ronton with you, you will not need them."

"What is a Ronton?"

"Slave fighter, a being without any purpose or desire except to obey and protect the Sens," replied Floo.

"The Sens?"

"The leaders of the Gants."

Amanda sighed and nodded. "Floo, our society is organized differently than yours. Yes, these people are my protectors, but they're not slaves, and they have many other tasks that they freely choose for themselves just as they chose this one. They're here because your people are known to be aggressive and dangerous. My companion thought it best.

"They'll accompany us today at the request of the commander of this ship. You will meet her soon. Come, this way."

She turned and led them out of the arrivals area. Floo noticed as Thirteen stepped between him and Amanda, then the deadly one that had killed so many then escaped them on Igen, moved in behind him. Floo was careful to make no sudden moves, yet he eagerly took in everything he could see.

When they arrived on the bridge his eyes opened wide with wonder. Unlike the great control room of Igen, this control room was alive with activity. Each of the seats had a body in it, a person working in tasks unknown. Two others moved about, overseeing the workings of the many. One approached them.

Smiling, Amanda turned to introduce them. "Floo, this person is Captain Rhonda Moore. The ship we are on is called the Reacher, and Captain Moore is her commander."

"It is a pleasure to meet your companion, Amanda."

"I'm not Vice-Admiral Drake's companion, Floo," smiled Rhonda. "I command this ship, the admiral, Amanda's companion, commands all the ships in our group. Come, let me show you around." She led them to one station with a flickering screen. The small man standing there smiled then stood back. "This is the sensor station. See this object here, this is another ship of our fleet, the Orca. This object here is your ship, Igen."

Rhonda gave them a quick lesson on how to work the controls then they moved on to the next station, engineering. Amanda was impressed as Rhonda took her time, explained each station and its main function, how it interacted with the others, and more.

Floo was utterly fascinated and thrilled as Rhonda let him ease the helm around and move Reacher slowly full circle about Igen and watch it on the big screen. He was completely unaware that the helm was actually isolated from the ship and that Commander Ortega was doing the maneuvering from the secondary station.

When the tour was over Floo's world view was changed forever. "Amanda, you say your people will teach us how to do these things, to control Igen and keep everything working smoothly?"

"Yes, but Igen will be different from Reacher. First our people must explore the workings of Igen, make all necessary repairs. We will teach you these things as we learn them. Together we can revive Igen. Will you allow us to help you? Will you grant us access to your bridge?"

"Bridge, like we saw today, the main room of control?"

"Yes."

"How will you learn these things?"

"First some of our people will go there, those with experience in such things. Linsey will learn how to speak with Igen, learn what Igen can teach her about the Growes and Gants and how they came to be. With this knowledge, others can then begin to understand how to help Igen heal. Will you allow this?"

Eelee gripped Floo's arm tightly. "Do it Floo, let them teach us. If we have the knowledge of control the Gants will never again be able to put us in the pens."

"We will allow this, Amanda. However, the Gants, may they choke on the meat, will surely attack us to prevent us for they have tried many times to re-take the room of full control. Will you send your Rontons to help protect us?"

"We won't be drawn into your war, Floo, but we will defend ourselves."

"What do you propose to do?"

Amanda turned to Twelve. "You were over there, Twelve, how would we defend the bridge without killing anyone?"

"Scatter blasters set on low should do the trick," replied the voice of the dangerous one beside Floo.

"Understood. Floo, we can travel directly onto your bridge and defend the entrance from inside. Is this acceptable to you?"

"It is."

"Then take Selea with you onto your bridge. When she calls, we can send our people over."

"Then that's what we will do. Send us home and when the light returns to Igen we will call again."

* * * * *

Once Floo and company were back aboard Igen, Amanda called a full meeting of the captains and Reacher's senior staff. "Everyone's here, Admiral."

"Thank you, Vice-Admiral Drake, the meeting is yours," smiled Jeannie as she sank into her chair.

Amanda nodded then began. "First, thank you, Captain Moore for that stellar tour of the bridge you gave our guest. It went better than I'd hoped and had the desired outcome. We've been granted full access to their bridge.

"However, we were warned to expect trouble from the Gants. I also noted that Floo was extremely wary of SUVI 12. For the next step I'd like to send Linsey and Moira over to learn what they can."

"They'll need security," said Jeannie.

"Send strikers," said Captain Sessas. "Send SUVI 12 too."

"Why send Twelve, Sessas?" asked Jeannie, a grin playing at her lips.

"Aliens fear Twelve, be more respectful."

"She's got a point," chuckled Captain Baris.

"Yes she does," agreed Amanda. "Rhonda, do you think Hal can spare his favorite gunner for this mission."

"He can," chuckled the Reacher's Chief of Security. "I'll let her know about the new assignment."

Amanda nodded. "Okay, so that's under control. Rhonda, he said they'd call when the light returns to Igen. Have sensors been tracking the night/day cycle on that ship?"

Rhonda reached for her comm. "Captain to Second Officer."

"Here, Captain."

"Anita, are we tracking the night and day cycle on the generation ship?"

"Just a minute ... yes, we've got that."

"Where are we in that cycle?"

"Their lights just dimmed. It'll return in nine hours."

"Great work, Anita, thank you. Moore out. There you go, Vice-Admiral. We've got about nine hours."

"All right, prepare your crews people and report to transportation in nine hours. Rhonda, ask Anita to keep an eye on the area of Igen's bridge, let me know if there is any extra activity there during their night cycle."

"Of course, Vice Admiral. You don't trust them?"

"No, I don't. Where the safety of our people is concerned, I don't trust anybody. Captain Morthel."

"Vice-Admiral?"

"I'd like Thirteen to go along on that security detail as well."

"I'll let him know immediately."

"All right, people, is there anything I've missed?" There was nothing. "Then we're good to go. I'll see you in Transportation in nine hours. Meeting adjourned."

* * * * *

Rayla found Twelve sitting by herself in the mess. "Hey there, how was the big tour today?"

"It was interesting. So, my precious girlfriend, tell me your big news."

"What makes you think I have news?" asked Rayla, a twinkle in her eye.

"I'm SUVI, I know things. Come on, share the news, you know you want to."

"We're going back to the alien ship, security force for Captain da Silva and Chief Engineer Duncan."

"I know, I've been assigned to that detail. Floo and I have history, the Vice-Admiral believes my presence will keep him respectful. Now stop trying to hold out on me and share the joy."

"I have no idea what you're talking about," said Rayla, fairly vibrating with excitement.

That made Twelve laugh. "You're busting to share something, you have a new uniform with a commander's insignia on it, and that tells me there's been action somewhere. You got a promotion, so what's the new job, commander of the strikers maybe?"

"Well damn, Twelve, way to spoil my big announcement."

Twelve reached across the table to grip her hands tightly. "Rayla, I'm so sorry, I ..."

"No, honey, no. I'm just teasing you. I knew damn well you'd figure it out, can't fool a hunter like you, you're way too observant for that. Yes, Billy got his transfer to Orca as the new Second of Security there. I got the promotion to lead the strikers. He starts his new job in two weeks so he's giving me the lead now but showing me the ropes as well."

"I can see that makes you happy. Congratulations."

"Thanks. Is something wrong? No, wait, SUVI, of course, don't hold rank, won't give or take orders, I get it. You've been assigned to my group, and I've been promoted to command it. We're all brand new trying to build a relationship and this could get weird between us ..."

"Easy, now, Precious, easy. I'll follow your commands on this hunt. You lead the hunt and I'll hunt with you. It'll be okay."

Rayla sighed and squeezed her hands again. "Why is it never easy?"

"Couldn't tell you, girl," chuckled Twelve, "but it never seems to be."

"Twelve, I'm a bit scared here, how do we do this and not mess it up between us?"

"Captain da Silva and Commander Duncan seek the prey; our job is to watch and divert any garogs that could mess with them. You direct us in that."

"Did you ever hunt with other SUVI?"

"It was rare, but sometimes we hunted together when the caverns were low on meat."

"Is that how you did it?"

"Yes. Five would always lead us, seek the prey. We kept the garogs and such off her as she located the elusive Tatras. When the hunt was successful we kept the predators away until the meat could be gathered. Those were good days."

Twelve had a touch of a smile on her face and Rayla reached for her hand. "Tell me about that, the hunts with Five to lead you."

"Five always seemed to know where the prey was. We'd gather our spears then set out. Once we found them we'd watch them for several days before we made a kill. Five always said we should never make it seem too easy, so we'd watch and just enjoy the time together. Time together with no humans around making demands or playing with the pain collar controls. It was the closest thing to freedom a SUVI could know, and only the hunters ever got to enjoy it.

"So that's how we'll do this, my precious girl. Linsey and Moira will gather the prey, the rest of us will relax in the sun, keep a close watch, drive away anything that shouldn't be there, and just enjoy each other's company."

"Wow. Tell me what the admiral was like as a leader when you hunted."

"She always knew where the prey was but had First Prime convinced they were hard to locate," chuckled Twelve.

"As a leader? She never spoke a harsh word, or chastised anyone, we got too much of that from the humans. She gave you a task and trusted you to get it done. She was always watching though, and if you caught her watching you she always gave a word of encouragement or a nod of approval. Somehow you always wanted to please her and tried harder."

"Wow. I guess I need to change my style a bit."

"Oh?"

Rayla sighed and let her shoulders relax. "Yeah, I tend to push hard and in training, I demand more, both of myself and everybody else. That's my father's teachings at work, and maybe a bit of my resentments at work too."

Twelve didn't say anything, just squeezed her hands. Rayla sighed again and went on. "Dad is a strange character. He was so proud when

Kim was born, a son to carry on the name, his legacy. I was suddenly no longer interesting.

"I remember trying everything to get his attention again, but soon saw how hard he was being on Kim. Kim has no interest in being the tough guy like Dad. The more Dad drove him the more Kim hid behind Mom.

"I started getting in the middle, telling Dad to back off, trying to protect Kim. We fought a lot after that, and I guess I developed a bitter attitude. I push myself hard and expect everyone else to do the same.

"The thing is, honey, the strikers have to be tough, to push themselves hard in training. One day that training could keep them alive."

"As it did for you on Igen when you escaped the Growes."

"Yes. Those people are tough and fast. I couldn't fight them without the new armor, but even with that I'd be dead if I hadn't been able to fight hard and keep it up. Now it just got tougher. How do I convince them to push harder without making them resent me?"

"Like Five used to do," grinned Twelve. "Push them hard to train, then on the hunt trust them to get it done yet stay watchful and help them as needed."

"That's good advice, and I'll follow it. Help me, keep me on the straight and narrow?"

Twelve gently squeezed her hands again. "My precious girl, I will do all in my power to support and help you. I promise.

"Now, we'd better get some rest. Tomorrow will be an interesting day."

Rayla nodded. "Walk me home?"

"I'd be delighted."

She rose and took Rayla's arm. As they walked along Twelve felt Rayla gently steering her to a different path. "Rayla, honey, where are we going?"

"Your quarters, more privacy there."

"Oh? Is this part of the relationship thing?"

"Yeah, could be I guess. I just want that cuddle session you've been promising me. I want to cuddle into your arms and stay there until the alarm goes off."

"I think I'd like that," smiled Twelve as she put her arm around Rayla's waist and gently pulled her closer.

Betrayal

Tonts and Keta with four companions approached the secondary bridge, or the small room of controls as they knew it. As they neared the door the translation device on Keta's tunic spoke, carrying to them the words of the two human engineers inside.

"What do you think, Jean? Are we likely to be assigned to the main bridge team?"

"What do you mean?"

"I heard some of the others talking. Apparently, the leader of the Growes was given a tour of the bridge on Reacher. In return he's invited us to investigate the bridge on Igen. You know, the place they call the one room of control."

"Really? That would be a great assignment all right. The Gants have a good grasp of what can be done from here, and there's not a lot more we can do until we get to the main bridge or main engineering. We could get lucky. Are we going to be teaching the Growes too?"

"Apparently that's the plan. I'm not sure what the Vice-Admiral has for an overall plan, but I'm really excited about what Captain da Silva will learn here."

"If you're so all fired interested in how other species evolved, how did you end up in engineering?"

"There were no other species to study back then," he chuckled.

* * * * *

Their conversation drifted away onto other topics, but the Gants had heard enough. They withdrew and called a meeting of the top leaders of the Sens. Tonts related what they'd heard.

"No, they can't do that," exclaimed one. "If the Growes learn how to work the room of full control they'll kill us all."

Several others agreed, but Tonts called for caution. "Let's not do anything rash," he said as he restored order. "The outsiders have helped us and taught us much. So what if they teach the Growes, with what we've learned we will be able to counter any aggressive move they make. We need to be patient."

That idea didn't go over so well, and it took him a while to regain control. Finally things began to settle down. One man stepped forward. "Sen Jara?"

"Tonts, you have led us for a long time and led us well, but we've slowly been pushed back and reduced in numbers, both by the war and the lack of food. We have an opportunity here, but you refuse to grasp it."

"Explain."

"Now is the time to strike. The Growes will gain the room of full control unless we do something and do it swiftly."

"Jara, we dare not attack the Growes now. They'll be guarding the room of full control with all their forces. We must wait and allow the outsiders to learn what they can. They've promised to teach us, and they have. If we ask them to teach us what they learn from that room, I'm certain they will.

"We'll be patient, but Keta can contact Amanda when the light returns to Igen, ask her if they will share with us the knowledge they gain there." With that pronouncement the meeting broke up and Tonts went to his rest. Jara didn't.

They came in the night while Tonts and Keta slept. They were taken, restrained, and forced into a small room where the two humans from the room of control were lying unconscious. One was bleeding badly. "They taste foul," snarled Jara as he jerked the comm badge from Keta's shoulder. "Now, how do these things work?"

He tried several times and got no response. In frustration he passed it back to her. "Use that thing, call the outsider. Tell her she answers to me now."

"No."

"You will do it, or I'll kill and eat Tonts before your very eyes. I've had enough of these weak ways. Our people fail and perish under his leadership, his lack of courage. I'm in control now; do as I say or he dies."

Reluctantly, Keta reached for the comm.

"Tell her I won't deal with a servile companion; I want to speak with their true commander."

Keta nodded and called Amanda.

* * * * *

Amanda was just waking up when the call came. "Keta to Amanda. Keta to Amanda, please talk to me."

"I don't like the sound of that," said Jeannie.

"Nor do I," muttered Amanda as she reached for her comm which lay on the floor. "Amanda here, Keta. How can I help?"

"Amanda, Tonts and I have been captured as have two of your own people. The new leader of the Gants is Jara. He will only speak with your companion and demands to do so now, or he will kill the two people he captured from the room of control."

Jeannie's eyes were glowing amber as she leaned across Amanda's shoulder and spoke. "Put him on."

At the sound of that voice filled with command and barely controlled rage, Jara swallowed hard. He shook it off and puffed himself up then spoke. "I have captured two of your people as well as the traitors you enlisted, Outsider. You will hold all your people back from the room of full control or they will all die. You will then assist me and my people to regain the room of full control and teach us what we must know to control the Growes and all of Igen. Fail me in this and your people will die."

Jara actually began to tremble in fear as she replied to his demands. "Hear me well, Gant. I have no love for you or your kind, that's why my companion deals with you. I will make you this promise, harm one of my people and I personally will come for you. Pray I do not have to do that."

He tried to bluster something, but the comm had gone dead. Jara swallowed hard once again. He had made a bad mistake and he knew it. He might have been able to negotiate with the companion, but not that one. Ah well, he'd made his play and now could only see it through and pray for an outcome he could live with.

Amanda waited for Jeannie's eyes to return to green. "What do you want to do here, sweetheart?"

"That's up to you, sweet Mandy. This is your assignment, your task, and I have every confidence you can handle it. I just wanted to give him something to think about. This is your task to deal with."

"Then I'll get to it. Vice-Admiral to the bridge."

"Rhonda here," came a yawning voice in response.

"All captains and your senior staff to the bridge meeting room ASAP."

"On it." Rhonda was wide awake now, and within moments the requested personnel were hurrying to the bridge.

"Looks like we're all here, Vice-Admiral."

"Thank you, Captain Moore. People, we have an emergency. There's been a coup in the Gants faction aboard the Igen. Two of our engineers have been taken hostage as have the former leader and his companion.

"Captain Sessas, your job is to retrieve them."

"I go," replied Sessas as she rose and hurried out of the room.

"People, this changes things."

"Are we still going ahead with the plan to access their main bridge?"

Amanda turned to face her former captain, her lover's grandfather. "Yes, Captain Baris, we are. However, I mean to be a bit more aggressive about our defenses. When Floo calls I'll inform him of what's happened, caution him to keep his forces on alert. I'll also ask Captain

Moore to assign a strong security detail to safeguard our people as they explore that bridge."

Rhonda nodded and turned to Hal White, her Chief of Security. "Hal, make it happen."

"I'll send the crew of EX4," he grinned. "I'll lead them myself."

"Excellent."

"May I ask your plan, Vice-Admiral?"

"Of course, Captain Baris. The plan is to help them learn how to sustain their own ship and population, as it was in the beginning. That will mean bringing them into a truce and learning to work together. I believe I can do that with Floo and Tonts."

"But not the new guy?"

"No, this Jara took control by force and made demands, one of which was to only deal with the admiral and not her lackey. Jeannie explained to him what would happen if she had to get involved. I think he'll be a bit more cautious from now on."

"So, you're going to try to reinstate the original leaders?"

"Yes, Captain Baris, I am. These people need to settle their differences if they hope to survive, and this man has no interest in that. He wants to dominate them all, and that means the Growes in holding pens to be slaughtered for food, ultimately the end of his species."

"Admiral, how do you feel about this?"

"Grandfather, I have every confidence that Amanda will find the solution here, for she holds the main objective at the forefront of her thoughts, help them repair their ship and survive."

"So you won't get involved?"

"Only if Amanda asks me to. Grandfather, I trust the Vice-Admiral to handle this. It is easily within her abilities. I gave her the task and only asked to be kept informed as to her progress. This is leadership by the book of Frank Baris, Captain of the Reacher, the ship that rescued me from slavery. I'm just following your example here."

Captain Baris chuckled and shook his head. She had him, that was exactly what he'd advised her when she was first a new captain.

"Vice-Admiral, I've just been informed the Retriever has launched," said Captain Moore.

"She didn't waste any time," said Captain Morthel.

"Sessas never does," chuckled Captain Ka'Ron of the Kreenon.

"Well, since Sessas is on the job I should get to work too," said Amanda. The meeting broke up and Amanda set to work.

* * * * *

Twelve grunted awake as a muttering Rayla reached across her to silence the comm. She kissed Twelve's cheek then rolled across her and fled to the facilities. "This is way early, something big must be up," she sighed as she rose from the seat to wash her face.

"Ah, seat's still warm," chuckled Twelve.

"I aim to please," grinned Rayle as she struggled into her new uniform.

"And you do succeed, my precious girl. Let's go."

They reached the ship to find the rest of the crew assembling. The captain was already there. "Kumar, everybody here, launch ship."

"Aye, Captain. Crew is aboard, we have clearance, launching now. Ship is in space."

"Well done. Crew, asshole go crazy, capture two engineers, Gant leaders, threaten Admiral Sorenson. Our job, get captives back. Rayla, you lead strikers. What want to do?"

Wide eyed, Rayla froze for only a moment then snapped back. She swallowed hard then spoke. "Okay, we have two SUVI hunters with us and our own super intuitive Twenty. Transport us aboard near that control room. Twenty, see if you can point us in the right direction. SUVI hunters, once you get on the trail the humans will keep the enemy off you to let you work.

"As soon as the SUVI hunters find them for us the humans will take our people back. Are we ready?"

"All ready," grinned Twenty, patting the war hammer at her side.

Rayla nodded. "Send us over," she said as she stepped onto a transport pad.

* * * * *

While Sessas was transporting her strikers over to Igen, Amanda was trying to contact Floo. "Amanda to Selea. Amanda to Selea, please respond."

A sleepy voice replied to her call. "Amanda?"

"Selea, is Floo anywhere near where you are?"

"What? No. Floo and Eelee are at their rest."

"You must warn them, Selea. Another man has taken the leadership of the Gants by force. He may attack you. Warn Floo then ask him to contact me."

"Yes, Amanda. I go."

* * * * *

The strikers arrived on Igen in a flash of light, the immediate area was empty. Rayla poked her head around the corner then pulled back. "Three on guard at the control room. Twenty, any idea if our people are in there?" Twenty tilted her head and let her eyes go out of focus for a moment, then she shook her head. "Which way?"

Another moment then Twenty pointed. "Twelve, take the lead."

"Yes, Ma'am," grinned Twelve as she led off in the direction Twenty had indicated. She soon got the scent, human scent, the scent of human blood.

They proceeded cautiously, all eyes roaming over the corridors ahead and to the side. Twelve led them down several different corridors before holding up her hand for silence. She motioned with her hand and Thirteen slipped ahead of her and around a corner.

A moment later they heard a soft bird call and Twelve grinned as she led them out again. They kept to the main hallway and Thirteen joined them. Rayla glance down the side corridor to see a dead Gant lying against the wall, his own crude blade protruding from his chest.

A bit further on Twelve stopped and signaled Rayla to come up. "They're close. The scent is strong now."

She nodded and pulled a small periscope from her pack. Carefully working it around the corner she took a good look then withdrew the instrument. "There's a door," she said quietly, "with five on guard. This must be the place. Billy, Artha, Singen, take them out."

The three heavily armed fighters leaped around the corner, opening fire with their blasters. The five guards were hurled down the hallway, tumbling head over heels. "Nicely done," grinned Rayla as she glided up beside them.

The door refused to answer her efforts to open it. With a snarl she stepped aside and motioned with her hand. SUVI 20 danced into the space Rayla vacated, her war hammer arcing through the air at great speed. The door collapsed inward at the impact and the strikers leaped through. Another five guards were inside.

The Gants attacked instantly, but the strikers had switched from blasters to stunners. Three Gants went down instantly, Thirteen grabbed another and threw him through the now open door, and Rayla used the butt of her weapon to brain the last one that was trying to rip Artha's head off. "Damn," grunted the woman as she struggled back to her feet. "Thanks Boss."

"Pleasure," grinned Rayla. "Billy, we get them all?"

"We did, Ray, but this man's hurt bad."

"Everybody else okay?" There was a round of, "All good here," from the group.

"Call for transport, out, Billy."

"Aye, Commander Mills. Strike Force to Retriever."

"Here," came the voice of the captain.

"We got them all, Captain. Bring us home."

"Understood. Prepare for transport."

"Hurry it up," said Rayla. "We've got incoming." As she spoke she opened fire with her blaster, sending several of the new attackers flying. She and her strike force disappeared from the Igen.

They arrived on Retriever and began to slowly strip off the war gear. "Well?" asked the Captain as the two medics worked on the injured man.

"Captain, it looks like they tried to eat him alive," said one medic as he continued to apply pressure while his companion cleaned the jagged wound.

"They did," agreed the female engineer who'd been working with the injured man. "Apparently he tasted bad."

"We've got him stabilized, but I'd like to get him into medical on the Reacher."

"Transport him over. Rayla, report."

"Aye, Captain Sessas. We arrived at an empty corridor, SUVI 20 gave us a direction, Twelve took up the hunt, and Thirteen cleared away the opposition until we found the place where they were holding them. The strikers cleared away the guards, Twenty opened the door for us then the strikers cleared out the guards from inside. We got our people plus the Gants requested, then transported home."

"Any dead Gants?"

"One for sure, Captain, but no more."

"Billy, your assessment?"

"Commander Mills was the right choice to lead the strikers, Captain. She assessed the skills of her assets, assigned the tasks, then watched over us while we worked. I feel confident I can transfer to my new post with a clear conscience."

Sessas gave her hissing laugh. "Billy say good job, Rayla. You find new striker to replace him."

"Yes ma'am, thank you, Captain."

"What will happen to us now?" asked Tonts.

"That for Vice-Admiral to decide. Kumar, take us home."

"Retriever returning to Reacher, aye Captain."

"Sessas to Vice-Admiral."

"Amanda here."

"Success. Have people, injured, transported to Reacher. We returning with prisoners."

"Prisoners?"

"Former leaders of Gants."

"Good, you got them out. Thank you, Captain Sessas. Sessas, they're not prisoners, they're friends. I'll meet your ship when you arrive. Amanda out."

"Friends?" mused Sessas. "Sessas not so sure. Take off restraints, give food. Rayla watch."

"Aye, Captain," replied Rayla as she knelt to get the binding off Keta.

* * * * *

While the strike force was tracking down and rescuing the captured humans, Floo and the Growes were preparing for a battle. He'd taken Amanda's warning to heart and immediately sent out scouts. The rest of the Growes were awakened, the old, young, and infirm, were moved deeper into the jungle with a strong force to guard them. The rest prepared to ambush the advancing Gant force. In the midst of that madness, Floo disappeared in a flash of light.

"What the ... how???"

"Relax, Floo, we brought you over so I could talk to you."

"What? Now?"

"Yes, now," sighed Amanda. "There's someone I want you to meet. With luck he'll be here soon."

"Who is this one you want me to meet?"

"Tonts, leader of the Gants," replied Amanda.

Shocked, Floo leaped at her, but was felled by a blow that stunned him. A female with glowing eyes was between him and Amanda. He shook off the cobwebs, but remained on the floor where he'd fallen. There was something about this new one. Floo could feel the power that emanated from her and felt true fear for the first time in his life.

"Floo, this woman is my companion, the one you wanted to meet. She won't hurt you if you don't do anything aggressive."

"Again you people amaze me. You have a Ronton for a leader."

"I was once a slave, yes, but no longer. Know this, I have fought and killed many animals far more dangerous than you. Remain respectful of Amanda and our people, do this and we will be respectful of you and your people as well.

"For your information, I personally believe your cause is just. However, Igen is dying, as are her people, all of them. Amanda has a plan to prevent this, to help you all learn to care for your ship, for all to survive for many more generations. I strongly suggest you work with her."

Floo slowly regained his feet and nodded and offered his hands. "There is no need for restraints; I'll be watching."

He nodded and let his arms fall to his sides. They had not harmed him yet and this one promised they wouldn't. He'd reacted instinctively and nearly got himself killed; all his people killed. This leader would show no mercy if her companion were harmed. He could hardly wait until the Gant arrived to see what would happen.

It wasn't a long wait. Others soon arrived with the two Gant leaders. At first sight of Floo they both stiffened, but the female caught the male by the arm and kept him in check. Suddenly Tonts sneered and pointed at Floo. "I must thank you, Amanda, both for the rescue and for providing us with food."

Floo flinched at that, but a hand fell on his shoulder, and he froze. He looked around to see the leader wink at him then release him. He turned back as Amanda began to speak.

"Tonts, Keta, welcome. You're here as my guests, so is Floo. I'll ask you to be civil to each other while you're here on Reacher. Now, everyone please sit down." Amanda smiled as she sat and indicated they should as well. They sat, eyeing each other carefully. "Tonts, tell us what happened."

He sighed and almost melted into his chair. "It was going well. Your people came and corrected our mistakes, taught us how to work many of the controls, what they do and why. Sadly, some of our people overheard your people talking among themselves about the Growes granting you access to the main room of control.

"They came to me and wanted to mount an attack at once, believing you had betrayed us. I doubted that, but suspected you offered the Growes the same thing you gave us, help and knowledge of the workings of Igen."

"Yes, we did."

"My people are afraid that, with such knowledge and access to greater control, the Growes will kill us all. I forbid the attack, saying I would contact you, to ask if you would teach us the things you teach the Growes. Jara didn't like my way; he never does. He secretly formed a group; they captured two of your people as well as Keta and me. He then took full control of the Gants."

"Can you regain that leadership if we put you back inside Igen?"

"I don't know, Amanda. Perhaps. Some will follow me; others will follow Jara. What will you do now? Why have you brought that here?"

"His name is Floo, Tonts, and he's the leader of the Growes. He's here at my invitation, to listen to my plan even as you are."

"You seem to be quite docile, Growe. How did they manage to convince you to listen to reason?"

Floo chuckled as the translators spoke the Gant's words. "I had a conversation with the supreme leader of these people, Gant. She can be most persuasive. It will cost us nothing to listen, and we may learn how to save Igen."

Tonts started to reply, but Keta grabbed his arm and pointed to Admiral Sorenson. A few whispered words and he settled back. "I agree. It costs nothing to listen, and much can be learned. Little is learned in a battle."

"On that we agree," said Floo. "Amanda, please tell us your plan."

She smiled and began. "There is much to be learned here, first by us, then by you. We must learn what Igen can tell us, then you must learn this and then learn how to nurture Igen. Above all else, you must learn to work together."

That caused a fuss and they started to rise, but Jeannie's hand on Floo's shoulder settled him down. Tonts felt the power of the grip on his own shoulder and looked up to the glowing amber eyes of SUVI 12.

"Be wary of that one, Gant. I have fought her before and survived, many didn't."

At Floo's words, Tonts sat back, uncertain. "As I said," continued Amanda, "you have to work together if Igen is to survive."

"We will not willingly submit to the pens," snarled Floo. "We will never willingly nourish the Gants; may they choke on the meat."

"I agree, Floo," said Amanda. "We must find an alternate food source for them. Tonts, if we can find an alternate food source for your people, will you consider my plan?"

Keta nudged him and slowly he nodded. "Floo, if the Gants no longer hunt Growes for food, will you consider my plan?"

Jeannie patted his shoulder again and he chuckled as he nodded. "Yes, Amanda, my advisor here believes your plan to be worthy. If the

Gants no longer hunt us we'll consider the plan. However, it may be somewhat difficult to convince my people of this."

"On that we agree," sighed Tonts.

"Then you both have much work to do," said Amanda. "We will now send you back to your people to let them know what we propose. Floo, my people are ready to investigate the bridge on Igen." She passed him a strange object then one to Tonts. "Carry these with you. With these we can contact you and you us."

"Like mine, Tonts, here," said Keta as she fastened the comm unit to his collar.

"It works like the one you gave Selea?" asked Floo.

"It does," replied Amanda. "Come, we'll take you to transport and send you home. Tonts, regain control and hold your people back from fighting for now. Floo, let us on to the Igen's bridge then keep most of your people back, our people will defend it." With that she led them out and to the transport room. The plan was in motion.

Gaining the Bridge

Rayla stomped her foot in frustration, the door wouldn't open. She'd gone with the team to hand over the rescued people to Reacher Security then gone straight to Twelve's quarters, but the door wouldn't open. "Twelve, are you in there? Twelve?" She got no answer.

"Dammit. Computer, locate SUVI 12."

A voice from the walls replied to her inquiry. "SUVI 12 is in the bridge briefing room."

"The briefing room? I wonder what's going on. Ah well, guess I'll go see if I can round up a replacement for Billy." Feeling disappointed, she walked back to the ship Retriever and accessed the applications for striker. She found and talked with an eager young man, a grounder, but he'd been training with them, and she was impressed with his enthusiasm.

Once she'd spoken with him and confirmed his post, Rayla returned to Twelve's quarters, but she still wasn't there. "Ah to hell with it, I'm beat, guess I'll give it up and go home." She returned to her own quarters and went to bed.

Kim had seen her enter, but wisely hadn't spoken. Once she'd retreated to her own room he quietly enquired of Twelve's whereabouts. The computer directed him to EX4. Carefully entering the silent ship he looked all around, but saw no one. Twelve's soft voice startled him.

"Up here, Kim." Kim peered up into the gun turret and saw Twelve sitting at the controls. "I assume you're looking for me."

"I am, yes. Are you getting ready for war?"

"No," chuckled Twelve. "I often come here to think."

"Oh? Sorry, I'll leave you to it."

"No, stay. You sought me out, something must be on your mind."

"Yeah, you're right there. Rayla didn't come home last night; I just assumed she stayed with you."

"She did."

"Yes, well, she came home tonight looking like her world had fallen apart. Did the mission go bad on her?"

"No, actually it was a clean hunt. Rayla's a good leader, smart, careful, cool under stress. She excelled on that mission."

Kim sighed. "Then I guess it was you guys. I'll just mind my own business and go away now."

"Kim, is she sleeping now?"

"Yes."

"Okay, I'll talk to her when she wakes."

"Dare I ask what happened, Twelve?"

"I have no idea. She led the strikers for the hand off of captives and rescued people, I cleaned up the gear then was called to the briefing room by Five. She felt my presence would help keep everyone respectful. Once that meeting was over I returned to my quarters, but Rayla wasn't there.

"I checked and she'd been there twice but couldn't get in. I'd neglected to grant her access. I checked at the mess, and she wasn't there either, so I came here."

"Why didn't you come to our quarters?"

"You might have been sleeping, besides, she looked angry on that last security clip. That gave me a turn, so I came here to ponder my options."

"Ponder your options, I don't understand."

"You know the history of the SUVI?"

"I do, yes."

"Then you can understand my reaction to an angry human female, a woman who has expectations of me and I didn't meet them. I know things here are different from the caverns, but I still had a strong reaction, and I didn't like it."

"Are you going to break it off with Rayla?"

Twelve sighed and leaned back in the gunner's seat. "No, only she can do that now."

"I don't understand."

"I'm SUVI, instinctively I've chosen a mate, I can't undo that instinct. I can and will keep away from her if she asks me to, but I'll never initiate that rift; it would tear the soul out of me. No, no I'm just trying to understand what I need to do to make things right with her."

"My gods, Twelve, that instinct could give someone a terrible power over you."

"It could, and we all know it, so we avoid the mating possibilities, but as you know, a number of us have failed in that. It surprised me how powerful it was the first time we met on Igen."

"Wow."

"So, any advice that might help me make it right for her?"

Kim patted her arm and smiled. "Tell her what you just told me. Yes, that instinct will give her a great power over you, but I know my sister. She'll never abuse that, and she'll go all protective over you and all the SUVI.

"She was tired, and I'm sure impatient when she couldn't access your quarters, but that's all you saw on her face, Twelve. My big sister is mad for you." Again he patted her arm then turned and walked away.

Twelve sat lost in thought for a while longer. Finally she returned to her quarters. "Computer, grant full access to these quarters to Commander Rayla Mills."

"Acknowledged."

Twelve stripped off, showered, then went to bed. She was keenly aware as the door opened and Rayla crawled into the bed beside her and took her in loving arms. "Kim told you about our little talk?"

"He did. My darling Twelve, I wasn't angry with you, I was just upset and scared that you'd changed your mind."

"Rayla,"

"Hush now, let me cuddle you to sleep."

"There's something I should tell you ..."

"I know, honey, you're stuck with me forever, my world is blessed. I know what my anger would do to you, my love, but I promise I'll keep a reign on that. You'll have to help me."

"Yes, my precious girl, I'll do everything I can to help you."

"Go to sleep now."

* * * * *

"Floo, thank Igen you're back. Are you harmed?"

"No, Eelee, I'm unharmed. I was taken aboard the outsider's ship again, and this time I met the supreme commander of their people. She admitted she believes our cause is just, and she wants to help us. I also met the leader of the Gants. The supreme leader soon took the arrogance out of him, may he choke on the meat."

"The leader of the Gants, why was he there?"

"For the same reason I was, to hear Amanda's plan to save Igen and her people. The plan has three parts. Part one, the outsiders come to the room of full control to learn as much of Igen as they can. Part two, they teach us and the Gants what they've learned. Part three, all the people of Igen work together to save her."

"What? No? We'll never submit to the pens," came several voices at once.

"Yes, and I made it clear that we would never willingly nourish the Gants, may they choke on the meat. Amanda believes they can find another food source for the Gants."

"Their leader agreed to this?"

"He agreed to consider it, as did I."

"You did? Why?"

"Imagine, if you will, spending our days nurturing Igen instead of hunting and being hunted by the Gants. Amanda believes this is the only way to save Igen, and I'm starting to agree. There are so few of us now, and our encounters with the outsiders cost us a number of our best fighters. No, this could be the one chance to end this madness."

"This is a big risk, Floo, but maybe you're right. We can learn much here that could help us even if the outsider's plan fails," said Eelee. "What do we do now?"

"We pull everybody back from the room of full control. I'll stand at the door alone so the outsiders will know where to find it."

"Floo, no, what if the Gants attack? You can't ..."

"Be at ease, Eelee, be at peace. You will lead our hunters to the narrow passage that leads to the room of control, hide yourselves, and if the Gants come finish them." She grinned at that then set out, the rest of the gathered fighters following close behind. Floo went in the opposite direction.

* * * * *

While Floo was organizing his people, Tonts was having a more difficult time as he faced Jara. A dozen or more stood beside Jara, but an equal number of the Gants stood at Tonts' side. The meeting was tense and Tonts was afraid it could explode. His people would destroy themselves before ever hearing the outsider's plan to save them all, to save Igen.

"Think, Jara. Just for a moment stop and think. The outsiders came and took back their people. They released me and returned me to Igen. You greatly angered the supreme leader of the outsiders; she'll kill you on sight. Just be patient for now and let me deal with this.

"The outsiders have a plan to save Igen and all her people."

"You mean to put us all in the pens. No, I'll keep up the fight, it's better to eat than be eaten."

"The outsiders don't eat the meat of sentient species unless they have no other choice, Jara. They'll help us find another food source. I was on their ship; they gave us food that wasn't meat. Both Keta and I as well as her Ronton have eaten this food.

"This knowledge alone is invaluable to us. More young will survive, aging hunters will no longer have to submit themselves to the nourishing of others." That caused a buzz of conversation in those gathered around, and Jara fairly trembled with impotent rage. He was losing his grip on command, and he didn't like it.

He turned and stomped away, his most trusted followers close behind, but most people stayed behind. "Tonts, tell us more of this plan to save Igen."

"It will be hard for us, but if we work at it, we can succeed. The outsiders are even now in the room of full control. They will teach both Gants and Growes what they learn there. They'll also have people working on finding a new food source for us, for they believe the Gants and Growes must work together if Igen is to survive."

"What? No ..."

"Yes, my people, listen to me. Long ago this was the way of things. When Igen was strong, all people had a purpose, all people worked together to maintain Igen. This much we learned from the small room of control once the outsiders helped us. If we're to survive we must learn to do this again. Jara knows this, and it disturbs him greatly."

"I agree," sighed another man. "Jara will never work beside a Growe; he'd kill it in a heartbeat and eat the liver."

"I know," replied Tonts.

"So what's the answer?"

"We watch, we learn, and we keep a close eye on Jara."

"Tonts, you know he'll try to cause more trouble with the outsiders."

"Yes, that is my hope. The supreme leader of the outsiders emits a fearsome energy. She is a hunter like no other, she kept the Growe leader quite docile, and Jara has incurred her anger. With luck he'll do it again and she'll kill him for me, otherwise I'll have to do it myself."

"He has many followers, Tonts. The Growes will rejoice if we destroy each other."

"I know, if it comes to it I'll take a lesson from the teachings of Jara."

"Tonts?"

"I'll take him in his sleep even as he did me. He put rough hands on Keta, and he will die for that offence alone if for no other reason. For now, we do all we can to persuade his followers to our side. We must keep the peace until we learn what the outsiders can teach." The others nodded as they absorbed all he had told them.

* * * * *

"Amanda, can you hear me?"

"Amanda here, Floo."

"I stand alone at the door to the room of control. It is safe for your people to come over now."

"Understood."

A moment later several people arrived beside Floo. Five heavily armed security people followed by Linsey da Silva, SUVI 18, and Commander Moira Duncan. Floo pulled a cord with a key from around his neck and unlocked the door. It creaked as he swung it open. The lights came up as they stepped inside and a voice spoke in a language they could not understand.

"All right, Linsey," sighed Moira Duncan. "Do your thing and decipher that language then convert it to English if you can."

"Working," she replied in a sing-song voice. She waved her arms around and moved from station to station. "Come on, come on, talk to me. Make some noise so my buddy here can work out your language."

Linsey stomped her foot when she got no response. "So, it's going to be the hard way, is it. Fine." She began to fiddle with different controls.

"Linsey, what the hell are you doing?" asked Moira.

"Looking for a response, hopefully a captain's log," she replied as she sat in the plush seat on the raised dais and started poking at the switches on the arm of the chair. This time she got her reaction as a huge screen lit up with the face of a Gant in an impressive uniform. To her great delight it began to speak. "Yes! okay, keep talking, my friend, keep talking."

Obediently, it continued. A short while later they all smiled as the translator device began to change the words into English. It was indeed the captain's log. Linsey grinned as she threw the switch to shut it off. "All right, that's step one down. Now for step two, the really hard one."

"Step two?"

"Yes, Moira, step two, the written language. Once I've got that you can do your job and I can get busy compiling the history of this ship and hopefully the history of its people. This ship doesn't have an AI to help us, but maybe I do."

"Linsey?"

"My ship. If I can get enough samples of the written language, Friendship can help me work it out. That's how I got the language for the Wrax ship, should work here."

Moira chuckled at that. "Do your thing, magic woman. Get me that language; it'll make my job a lot easier."

"Easier. Of course, why not try the easy way." Linsey hopped down from the dais and went to the door, Floo was still outside. "Floo, can any of your people read?"

"Read? What does this mean?"

"Read. Understand the symbols, like these." She pointed to the faded symbols over the doorway. "To read is to understand the symbols and how they make different words when they are arranged differently."

"I know this one is "tec", this is "ack", and this is "og", but I know not what they mean."

"Might any of your people know more?"

"Perhaps old Oolf, the eldest of our people, but his mind wanders now, and others have to watch him."

"Okay, thanks anyway. I guess I have lots more work to do." Linsey went inside again and sat in the captain's chair, thinking. Suddenly she sat up straighter, a look of determination on her face. She made an adjustment on her translator then spoke, the machine translating her words into the ancient language. "Computer, print out last three entries, captain's log."

A blinking light came to life as an ancient machine began to hum. A rapid tapping sound was followed by pages of paper covered in printed words, appearing from a console at her right hand. Linsey gathered them up with a grin of delight. "Great, that worked. Let's go Eighteen, we've got work to do.

"Linsey to Friendship, transport Eighteen and I aboard." She and her companion vanished from Igen's bridge.

Moira was still trying to puzzle out some of the displays when they returned holding some sort of instrument. "What have you got there, Linsey?"

"It's the thingy we invented to translate for the strikers on the Wrax ship. We've converted the language for Igen. Just hold it over what you want to read, and it'll translate for you."

"Okay, but why not convert the language to English like you did for the Orca?"

"Amanda asked me not to. She says, and I agree, this language is the elder language of all the people of Igen, a part of their heritage. We need to learn it and teach it to them, give them back what was once theirs."

"Aye, that does make sense, but it makes my job harder."

"Sorry."

"No, Linsey, this is the right way. Can you make a few more of those things for my engineers? It would be a big help."

"Engineering on Reacher already has the specs and is working on them now. Should be ready in a few hours."

"Excellent," mused Moira who was already turning back to the display, the instrument in her hand. Linsey grinned and returned to the captain's chair. She attached a recording device to the chair then activated the captain's log once again.

It took her a while to find the original entry, but she did. Fascinated, Linsey realized her machine was working to translate the language. Obviously, the language had evolved over the millennia, the original being more akin to the current language of the Gants. She grinned with delight as the machine began to make the adjustment and she could understand the voice speaking to her.

"This is Captain Tontha Oothra of the life ship Igen. Igen was built and launched in the hope of preserving our species, to go forth into the unknown and find a place of safety for our people. We have five thousand Gantry to operate the ship and preserve the gene pool, another five thousand Growers and their stock to provide food for all.

"As Igen approaches the outer limits of the sun's reach I have cautioned the people to be frugal in their use of the Growers and their stock. We must maintain a balance or else all will starve or worse in a few generations.

"Our course is set for the nearest star system, and we expect to reach it in less than nine generations. I will surely not live to see it, but it is my hope my descendants will."

Linsey sighed as she moved on to the next entry. Most were just daily running reports of the voyage's beginning. She found where they lost sight of their native star and the days of mourning that followed. Eventually she came to the end of that captain's reign and the beginning of the next.

"Captain Tontha Oothra, logging for the last time. Later today I will hand off command to my grandson, Elthran Oothra, who will guide Igen from this day forward. I was barely halfway through my lifespan when I assumed the mantle of Captain. Now age and infirmity have overtaken me. I pass the mantle to younger and more vigorous leadership."

The next entry was a different man facing her, and a different voice. "Captain Elthran Oothra, first log entry. For much of my life Igen has passed through the void, slowly making her way toward a distant pinpoint of light. I will never reach it, and if I turned back I wouldn't live long enough to get back to Ithica Prime.

"No, our ancestors have set us on this path, robbed us of a normal life in their blind ambition and idiotic adherence to an outdated religious fear of the unknown. So here we are, delicate creatures inside a hard shell, hurtling toward the unknown we can never reach. The mantle of leadership has fallen to me. I will do my utmost to keep all alive for as long as I can, then I'll pass the mantle to another."

Linsey poked her way through the entries and over the next few hours encountered two more captains, each in turn more bitter against the ancestors who had first set out on the mad voyage. Those people had condemned the untold generations to follow to live out their lives in the iron prison, as one captain had called Igen.

She was about to continue when Eighteen arrived and took her by the arm. "You need food then ten hours of sleep, sweet Linsey. I'm taking you home for a rest; you can return tomorrow and take up the quest once again."

"Yes dear," chuckled Linsey, "I hear and obey." As Eighteen led her away she noticed a different group of engineers busily working away at the different command stations. "How long was I in that chair?"

"Far too long, my love. Far too long." Eighteen called for transport and they returned to the Reacher.

The Past Revealed

As Linsey and Eighteen entered the mess they saw Amanda and the admiral with others at the head table. Jeannie motioned for them to join the group. "So, how's it going over there," asked Amanda as they sat down.

"Pretty smoothly, actually," replied Linsey. "We arrived without incident, got the language thing under control, then I got lost in the captain's logs. I found the original captain's log and had to work on a translation for that. They've been on that ship for a long time and the language has evolved from the original Gantry."

"Gantry?"

"Yes, Admiral, that's what they called themselves, the Gantry. They had a full complement of people at first, and an equal number of Growers, slave farmers as near as I can gather. The Growers raised livestock and plants to provide food for all. I'll be able to learn a lot more once I've had a few hours' sleep."

"What's the long term plan, Linsey?" asked Amanda.

"I want to see how it evolved for them, how they got off course, how the society broke apart into warring factions, and how the language has evolved from those events."

"That's a great idea," agreed Amanda. "Once you get it figured out, can you make up a basic history course for us to share with the Gants and Growes, help them understand where they came from, what they once were?"

"I thought you might want something like that, Vice-Admiral. I've already got it in the works."

"Linsey, you're the best. I'd better watch out or you'll have my job next."

"Oh no, no you don't, Vice-Admiral Drake. I'm keeping my job. I get to play with languages and meet all kinds of new people. I have a great ship and a crew who lets me play at being captain. I love my job. You just keep your eyes off my ship."

Everyone at the table was laughing and Amanda grinned. "It was worth a shot. Seriously, Linsey, you're amazing. Without your skill set we wouldn't have a hope with this project. Get some rest, Captain da Silva, you've got a mighty task awaiting you tomorrow."

Linsey smiled and relaxed back from her now empty plate. "Aye, Vice-Admiral, heading for the bunk as ordered." Eighteen rose and took her by the hand then led her away.

Amanda smiled and gently shook her head as Linsey and Eighteen walked away. "What is it, Mandy?"

"Linsey. I have no idea at all how she does what she does, but somehow, against all odds, she does it every time."

"Yes, she does," agreed Jeannie. "She has no idea just how invaluable she's become to the fleet, to us all. We were lucky to have found her."

"That's part of the Suvi-jean magic," grinned Amanda. "Somehow, my darling Admiral Sorenson, you always manage to find the right person for the key task to keep us all alive."

"I just look for the people who can get the job done and make me look good. Like you for instance, my bewitchingly beautiful companion."

"Woman, talk like that will get you everywhere," purred Amanda.

"I'm counting on it," grined Suvi-jean as she rose and offered Amanda her hand.

* * * * *

Eight hours later Linsey was back in the captain's chair aboard Igen. As the day wore on she learned more of how the ship Igen had evolved. The captain's logs revealed their entire history.

"Captain's log, day one of a new unintentional course. Last shift a small object struck Igen and penetrated the hull, destroying valuable technology and radically changing our course. We managed to seal the hull, and partially repair the tech, but the knowledge of how to properly repair it and restore our original course has been lost to us over time.

"As I sit here recording I can see the pinpoint of light that was our original target disappearing behind us. Our star charts tell us there is another star we might reach in eight generations or less, but the course corrections are difficult now. I have set people to study all they can find in the repair manuals, but I have little hope."

"Sweet mother of mercy," sighed Linsey as she moved to the next entry. A while later she found another.

"Captain's log, date unknown, but it was in my grandsire's time Igen lost her original path. We were actually making headway in changing course to another star when that idiot Janek went mad and killed a Grower who refused him extra meat. He actually cut off the dead man's arm and ate it. Sadly, he has many followers among the Sens, and I dare not execute him."

Linsey was paying close attention now. "Captain's log, five days from the murder of the Grower. The Sens are clamoring for justice as three dead Gants were found this morning. The idiots went hunting for Growers or Etacks for meat and they didn't care which. The Growers ambushed them and killed them.

"Result, we have lost our food source. The Growers have blocked off all access to the lower ship. I'm to meet with their leader in one hour. Hopefully I can resolve this peacefully."

"Captain's log, same day. The Growers have agreed to allow the Gantry food, but they will mete it out. They will no longer obey any command or directive from the Gantry, and there will be no retaliation for the dead men. We have a truce, and we have access to food. No more can I do at this time."

Linsey soon found another entry by the same captain. "Captain's log, day nine of the truce, Janek is dead, and I've been accused of the murder. I admit nothing, but his loss will ease the tension between us and the Growers. The man was utterly insane, and his loss is a boon to us all."

With another sigh, Linsey rose from the chair and stretched then returned to her task. She learned of the rift among the Gants growing stronger until there was a coup and a new captain appeared, a harsh and brutal man. His friends and supporters gained power and the rest of the Gants were enslaved to become warriors and hunters, hunters of Growers or Growes as he called them.

Two generations later the society was set with the Sens in full control and the rest of the Gants as servants. She could learn little of the Growes as they were only mentioned as the enemy. Slowly, piece by piece the Gants were pushed back, relinquishing territory in exchange for a supply of food.

While the new ways were evolving, most of the knowledge of operating a ship was lost, and Igen simply kept moving under the power of her original momentum. As near as Linsey could figure, that was several generations past.

"Captain's log, last entry. Our society has fallen, the war with the Growes has destroyed us all. We have gained a small portion of the food growing area, but at the cost of the bridge. I record this under the gaze of five Growes with spears. I am to be executed, the bridge is lost and in their control. I pray that one day someone will find these logs and understand what happened to our people. I now go to join my ancestors. End captain's log."

"Wow, holy crap," mused Linsey. "Okay, that's all I'll get here, now to talk to Floo."

"Floo?" asked Eighteen who had been at her side all day.

"Yeah, I doubt the Growes have anything like this log, but they must have lore speakers, right? They must have some sort of oral tradition of their history. It's worth a shot anyway."

"Indeed it is, my most cherished," chuckled Eighteen, "but it can wait for another day. You're falling asleep on your feet. I'm taking you home for a meal and ten hours' sleep."

"Can't argue that logic," smiled Linsey. "Take me away my super SUVI." Eighteen called for transport and they vanished in a flash of light.

Making it Work

While a tired Linsey was being guided home by her lover, Rayla sat nervously across the table from Twelve. She had barely spoken a dozen words for two days and the tension was palpable. "Twelve, are you angry with me?"

"What? No, girl, not at all."

"Then what is it? You've barely spoken a word for days, have you changed your mind? Second thoughts?"

"No. Stop this now, Rayla my sweet. You know that can't happen, not ever."

"Then what? This is making me crazy. Tell me what I've done so I can make it right."

Twelve reached across the small table and took her hands. "Please stop and let me try to explain. I confess I'm struggling a bit here, but not the way you think. Rayla, I'm not your father, my mood isn't anything you've done, and it's not your job to fix me."

"Fix you? Are you broken? Please talk to me, Twelve. Let me help."

"All right, I'll try, but you ... I don't want to upset you, and ..."

She got no further as Rayla stood up and pulled her to her feet. To Twelve's great surprise Rayla stepped into her arms and laid her head on her shoulder. "Hug me, hug me tight." Twelve was happy to comply. "Twelve, we're still new and trying to figure things out. I know you're stuck with me, but only if you want to be. That's my biggest fear, that you won't really want to be."

"That'll never happen, precious girl, and you know that."

"Yeah, my head does, but I still panic. It'll take time but I'll get past it. I just get scared when you're so quiet all the time."

Twelve hugged her tighter. "I'm so sorry to cause you distress. I'm just not a big talker, I guess. Never dared to try before, especially about what I was feeling inside, except with another SUVI and those chances were extremely rare.

"Understand me, I'm thrilled with what has happened here, that you, a full human, would actually want me, not as a thing, or a protector, but as a companion. I'm trying to get past the old trust issues, the instinctive fear of a human's touch, and more. I guess I got so quiet out of habit. If you don't speak you can't say anything wrong."

"Come here with me," said Rayla as she stepped back and gently pulled Twelve with her as she sank onto the sofa. "I won't hurt you, my love; just cuddle down here on my shoulder and let me hold you. Let's work this thing out together.

"So, here we are, a human who's an insecure mess and a brutalized SUVI with trust issues. We need to find a way through the strange pathways we've created for ourselves. Any ideas?"

"This is a good start," came a soft voice from her shoulder.

"Yes it is," she chuckled. "Honey, I know I'll never fully understand what it was like for you, the fear and loathing a human's touch must bring to you. This episode started when you flinched yesterday. I surprised you with a touch you didn't expect, and you reacted instinctively. My brain understands what happened and why, but the scared little girl inside me freaked out and withdrew into her shell."

"Yeah, and I drew back, afraid that you were angry that I'd pulled away. We're quite a pair, aren't we?"

"Yes we are. So, I'm feeling a lot better and more secure now. How can I help you to feel safer with me?"

"This is good," replied Twelve, still snuggled on Rayla's shoulder. "Next time I flinch away like that, just say, 'It's me, lover. Only me.' And I'll get a grip and know you aren't angry and that there's no threat."

The sweet interlude was suddenly interrupted by the ping of Rayla's comm. "Rayla here."

"Sessas. We pulling guard duty in Igen. Ten minutes to transport."

"On my way, Captain." Rayla sighed and released Twelve from her arms. "I'm so sorry, love, but duty calls. Looks like we get the night shift guard duty. You get some sleep, I'll get dressed."

"Go, you're on the clock," chuckled Twelve.

"Promise you'll miss me while I'm gone," said Rayla as she struggled into her uniform and stepped into the armored boots.

"I promise," smiled Twelve as she kissed the top of her lover's head. "Scoot now, don't want to be late."

"Scooting," replied Rayla as she kissed Twelve's cheek and fled the quarters. As she vanished from their rooms, Twelve sighed and rose from the sofa. She pulled on her jacket and stepped out the door.

A few moments later she met Kim coming the other way. "Twelve, you okay?"

"Sure, why wouldn't I be?"

"You two seemed a bit off your game lately, that's all. It's late and here you are walking away from your quarters, alone."

Twelve chuckled. "Rayla was called in. The Strikers have drawn guard duty on Igen."

"So, ...?"

"So I'm on my way to EX4 to swap with Two for the night shift, Two hates nights so it's a natural. This way Rayla and I can stay on the same shift. Relax Momma Kim, human-SUVI relations are a work in progress, but we're getting there. All's well on the home front."

Kim actually blushed and looked away. "Sorry, Twelve. I just can't seem to mind my own business. I'll try harder."

She smiled and patted his shoulder. "It's okay, my new brother. It pleases me that you care. I'm not offended. Now, off you go and get some sleep while the rest of us poor fools work the night shift."

"Yes Mom," he sighed as she continued on her way. "Anybody else would have slapped me down for poking my nose in like that. I seriously have to find a way to help you out, SUVI 12. My big sister has hit the jackpot at long last."

With that thought he returned to his own quarters which seemed empty now that Rayla had moved out. "Maybe I need to find a SUVI boyfriend," he grinned to himself as he settled down to sleep.

SUVI 2 was leaning against the hatch of EX4 when Twelve arrived. "Twelve, why aren't you in your quarters cuddled up to your mate?"

Twelve grinned. "The strikers got called in for a night shift of guard duty on Igen. I thought I'd see if you wanted to trade your night shift for my day shift tomorrow."

"Are you serious?"

"I am."

"I owe you, my sister. I gladly accept your sacrifice."

With that he gave her arm a friendly squeeze and walked away towards quarters. Twelve stepped inside and closed the hatch then climbed to her favorite perch in the gun turret. She sighed as she settled into the seat. Her natural reflexive instinct had nearly caused a rift between her and Rayla.

She'd have to curb that somehow, yet that very instinct to flinch at an unexpected touch had saved her life as a hunter on Elysium several times, and she had the scars to prove it. This was not going to be easy.

* * * * *

While Twelve was pondering her possible ways to get closer with Rayla, things aboard Igen were getting tense among the Gants. "Keta, what is it?"

"Quickly, Tonts, we must escape, they're coming."

"Who comes?"

"Jara."

Tonts needed no further urging; he grabbed his tunic and fled with her. It was close, but they made it out. A hard run through twisting corridors brought them to a large room. Many of their followers were there, waiting and heavily armed. Tonts had expected something like this and had been prepared.

"Is everyone ready?"

"Ready," came the full response.

One man tossed Tonts weapons, and they set out through a different door. "Hold the room as long as you can then retreat to position two," Tonts instructed one of those who were to remain behind. The man nodded as Tonts turned and fled through the exit. The man then locked it from inside.

Tonts soon caught up with the force led by Keta. "We're behind them, Tonts, but they are many. What do you want to do?"

"Hit them hard and fast then run. We go to position four, from there to seven, then back to two making certain we're not followed. That's how we must do this until we get lucky enough to kill Jara. Once he's dead the others will falter, and we can hopefully reclaim them to our cause."

"Tonts, are you so certain of this course of action? Are you utterly convinced of this plan the outsiders have hatched?" asked another voice.

"I am, Sen Ergath, I am. I have seen their world, the power they wield, and I have seen the leader of the Growes sit meekly listening, completely under the control of the Grand Leader of the outsiders.

"Sadly, people, I saw a glimmer of friendship between those two, and yet I sensed that mighty leader's disapproval of Gants. She approves of Amanda's plan, and I believe accepting this plan to be the only way for the Gants to survive now. The outsiders have come, people, the time of prophecy, of destiny, is upon us.

"Come, we must now hunt our own who have become the true enemy we face now." With that he led them out.

It didn't take long to find them, Jara's voice, raised in anger and frustration, could easily be heard. "They're still there," whispered Tonts. "Hit them hard then flee, you know the path. I'll throw my spear first; with luck I'll kill that traitor on the first throw."

It wasn't going to be that easy. Tonts leaped around the corner and brained the man who was supposed to be guarding the rear. He took three steps and hurled his spear. The lethal shaft sped toward its intended victim, but another had seen and pushed Jara out of the way. Shocked, he gazed at his savior choking out his life, the deadly spear lodged in his throat.

Gant war cries rang out and spears flew. Jara began shouting orders, forming his people into a tight defensive position. It took him several precious minutes to understand that the enemy had fled. "After them, get after them. Kill them all."

Jara's troops sped after the fleeing enemy, but soon rounded a corner and found themselves in a trap. They fought hard and managed to retreat out of that tight area, but they weren't followed. Closer investigation showed the passageway to be empty. The enemy had fled once again.

Jara was incensed, Tonts had led that attack and was free, free, and aware of the danger. Instead of catching him by surprise and killing him, Jara now had a fight on his hands, a fight he'd hoped to avoid. Tonts was a fierce warrior and a canny leader. Worse, Jara knew Tonts would avoid an open battle, but would hunt him personally. His attempted coup had gone seriously astray.

Tonts and Keta were among the last to arrive at location two. "All is well here?"

"It is, Tonts. Did you get him? Is Jara dead?"

"Sadly, no. Another pushed him aside and accepted my spear instead. I grieve for that man's life. How many others did we kill?"

"Four, and another badly wounded," came a different voice.

"How many did we lose?" asked Keta.

"Only one," replied the voice.

"As usual, your plan was successful, Tonts," said another. "So now what do we do?"

"More of the same, people. We avoid our elders, our young, and non-fighters. Jara wants to be the leader; he can feed them. Keta, contact Amanda, let her know what has happened, warn her to be wary." He sighed and let his shoulders slump. "Keta, ask her to warn the Growe leader as well. He should be prepared for increased attacks now."

Another stepped forward. "Warn the Growes? Tonts? How is Jara to feed the young and old if the Growes are expecting attacks and have time to prepare or hide?"

"With any luck at all, he won't be able to, Sen Ergath. That's when we appeal to the outsiders for some of their magic food for our vulnerable people."

The man nodded slowly. "And when we show we can provide for them and he can't, his people will turn against him and seek us out."

"That's the plan," sighed Tonts. "Get some rest people. When the light returns we hunt again. Sadly, it is our own we must hunt."

* * * * *

"Amanda to Floo," spoke the comm unit pinned to his tunic. Floo stopped what he was saying and looked at it, puzzled. Selea reached out to tap it lightly then nodded. "Floo here, Amanda."

"Floo, I've just heard from Tonts, the Gant leader. He asked me to warn you. His rival has attacked him, but was unsuccessful. Beware, that one may attack you as well for he hates all Growes."

"The Gant wanted to warn me?"

"He did, yes."

"Then he has embraced your plan?"

"I believe he's getting there nicely."

"Good to know. We will be watchful, Amanda. Thank you for the warning."

"Don't thank me, thank Tonts," she replied then she was gone.

"So the Gant leader will accept the outsider's plan?"

"I don't know, Eelee," sighed Floo. "Could be he just hopes we will defeat his enemy for him, but perhaps he can see the wisdom of the plan as well. Time will tell for sure, but for now we watch for the enemy and keep a close eye on our new allies as well."

Slow Going

"What is it, Admiral? What's bothering you?"

"Huh? Oh, this whole thing, Grandfather. This should have been an easy task, help these people make a few repairs then go about our business, but we've been here for weeks, and we're not halfway done yet. I'm starting to get a bit concerned about our own supplies, plus we're slowly using up our fuel. I ..."

"All captains to the bridge, all captains to the bridge. Passenger reps to the bridge. Admiral Sorenson, please come to the bridge briefing room."

"That was Mandy. We'd better get a move on, or we'll be in trouble." Captain Baris chuckled at that as he rose from his chair and followed his granddaughter from the mess. They arrived together to find everyone else already there.

"Looks like everybody's here, Vice-Admiral," said Captain Moore of the Reacher.

"Thank you, Rhonda. People, we have a developing situation on our hands. It's been brought to my attention that we've been sitting here, interstellar, for too long. We're starting to burn through our fuel supplies and more.

"We're here because we've offered to help the people of Igen, and they agreed to accept our help. We've interfered with their society, but we've also prevented them from destroying themselves. The problem is this, we're barely halfway finished. I have a possible solution, but I'd like your input into this.

"I'll admit the Admiral and I have spoken of this recently, but we didn't come up with anything concrete. With your permission, Admiral, I'd like to open this up to everybody."

"Granted, Mandy. Let's all put our heads together and see if we can figure something out."

Amanda smiled. "All right, people, opinions, options?"

"Is easy," said Captain Sessas.

Amanda smiled and Jeannie chuckled with delight. "Go ahead, Captain Sessas, what do you suggest we do here?"

"Reacher stay here, help Igen folk, keep Kreenon for guard. Orca take other small ships, go nearest system, gather supplies, fill holds, top up fuel, come back. Orca come back, Reacher, Kreenon, and small ship go, top up, then come back."

"I like it, Captain Sessas," smiled Amanda. "The admiral and I were thinking along those lines just last night. Anybody else?"

"I think Sessas has it," agreed Rhonda. "It's that or we abandon these folk to their fate. Who would have thought we'd find a primitive people on an interstellar ship halfway between systems?"

"It was pretty much a given, or so our people feared back when we were thinking about building one," said Captain Volkov. "There was a wave of relief when the super light engines were invented. It meant that we could avoid this particular trap."

"Trap?" asked Jeannie.

"Trap, Admiral," said Miriam Holbrooke. "The trap is, how do you keep the dream alive, and how do you educate the new generations, keep them excited about the dream, especially those born interstellar who will never live to see a star system. How do you avoid the natural resentments that will arise from this? Linsey's reports tell us this is exactly what happened on Igen."

"I understand," nodded Jeannie. "So, over the generations, the people of Igen have evolved new languages and ways of life. Amanda, my beloved, I fear I dropped an impossible task on your shoulders."

"Don't give up on me yet," grinned Amanda. "The plan here is to help them repair the ship and put them on the path of learning to maintain it. That's all we're here to do. If it were a smaller ship we could offer to tow it to a star system, but that's not the task we set for ourselves.

"We offered to help, and that's all we really can do here. In the end we'll have to leave them to their own fate, to create their own future and that of their people. We just want to help them find a way to survive.

"So, Admiral Sorenson, I like Captain Sessas' suggested plan."

"Then go with it Mandy."

"Jeannie?"

"This one is your baby."

"No it isn't, unless you pass it to me. Keeping the fleet supplied isn't part of my mission here, repairing Igen is."

"It was worth a shot," chuckled Suvi-jean. "All right, we go with the Sessas plan. "Sorenson to Probie."

"Probie is here, Admiral."

"Probie, I need you to scout out the next system, the one we were headed for when we found Igen. Report back as soon as you're ready."

"Understood. Probie is launching."

"Probe is away, Admiral," said Captain Moore as she glanced at her info pad.

"Good. Sheila, as soon as Probie reports that it's a go, take EX2 and the salvage ships with you, top up your fuel and supplies as best you can then return to us.

"Once the Orca returns, we'll shift our operations to the Orca so the Reacher can go resupply. If we're lucky we'll find everything we need there. Captain Moore, get a list of everything you'll need for EX2 so they'll know what is most important to look for."

"Already in the works, Admiral," replied Rhonda as she stopped tapping at the info pad and laid it aside.

"Yes indeed, the right woman for the job," grinned Jeannie.

Six days later the probe reported the next system was empty of artificial movement, one planet in the zone, plenty of ruins, but no signs of advanced life forms. Orca set out with EX2 and the salvage ships to see what they could find.

EX2 explored the planet while Orca and the small ships sat in high orbit, soaking up solar radiation for the fuel cells. After three days EX2 reported all was well, they'd found and gathered samples of several varieties of grains as well as located ancient ruins with an abundance of metals. The two salvage ships immediately set to work filling their holds with the grains, saving the metals for when they accompanied the Reacher when she came to refuel.

Meanwhile on Igen, things continued to deteriorate for her native people. Tonts continued to harass Jara's forces with sudden deadly surprise attacks. Jara, desperate for food for the troops as well as the elders and young, increased the raids on the Growes.

Being aware of what was going on, Floo had moved his people far back into the forested areas, only keeping a few scouts with him. An added bonus was Selea had accidently activated her comm and it wasn't Amanda, but Keta who answered. It was a stiff and constrained conversation, but the two did exchange names and a bit of information.

Once informed of what had happened, Floo and Tonts began to exchange information through the comms, coordinating their movements to avoid Jara's troops as well as to spy on him. Finally, one day Tonts was surprised when Selea contacted Keta with information of a food cache. When they found it there was also a strange form of meat there.

"Keta to Selea."

"Here, Keta."

"What is this meat-like food you left for us? I do not recognize it."

"There is a large creature that lives deep within the leaves. They are fierce and strong, but good meat. Floo sent out hunters to make a kill for you. It is safe to eat, Keta. It's what we eat, for if we only eat vegetation we sicken."

"Thank you, Selea, and thank Floo for us."

As Keta turned away to the food, Tonts was shaking his head. "Tonts?"

"It's a dilemma, Keta. Do I suddenly trust my lifelong enemy, take a leap of faith and try the meat?"

"I'll do it," said another. "I'm sorely wounded but you're not. The people need you, Tonts, but my days may well be numbered. I'll test the meat."

So saying, he cut a small portion and raised it to his lips. The others watched with bated breath as he slowly chewed, then swallowed. They all sighed with relief as a grin spread across his face. "Not bad at all," he said as he bit off another mouthful and began to chew contentedly.

That was all it took, the rest tucked in with a will. A short while later Tonts gazed around at his companions, all sitting back with contented smiles on their faces and their bellies full for the first time in a long time.

"Floo to Tonts."

"Here, Floo."

"We should have warned you, that meat will make you sleepy for a while."

"What???"

"There's something in it that makes you want to sleep. We never let a guard or hunter eat it before they go to work, they get too drowsy. Put a hungry person on lookout duty."

"Now you tell me."

"Sorry, Eelee just pointed that out to me. Your folk haven't had any of this before, it could have a strong effect."

"Good to know. Thank you." With that the comm went quiet and Tonts turned to the others. "You heard?"

"Yes," replied Keta. "He was right, all I want to do now is sleep."

"We should be safe here for a quick rest. Go ahead, but I'll remain on watch. Our Growe friend has given me much to think about."

"Tonts?"

"What do you think would happen if we put a large supply of this meat where Jara could find it?"

"We could sneak in and kill him in his sleep as he tried to do to us," she replied, nodding her head. "The idea does have possibilities." With that she settled back and closed her eyes.

* * * * *

While Keta was catching a nap and Tonts dozed on guard duty, Linsey got another breakthrough. She'd had little success with the elders of the Growes; their tales of younger days and stories their elders had related to them as children held no new information. She went back to searching for personal logs of the early crew.

Heavily guarded by both the strikers and the Growes, she'd poked around in some of the other areas of the ship under Growe control. Finally, in what must have been the crew quarters at one time, she hit paydirt. She found the personal log of the last medical officer.

"Chief Med Officer Krenth, personal log. I'm at my wit's end. The Growers have cut off our supply of meat. We know there are plenty of animals in the forested areas, but we can't get near them. Without meat our people will weaken, fall ill, and die a slow agonizing death. Somehow we must find a way to stop this futile war, or we will all perish."

"So that's it. I'd better call Amanda and let her know. Da Silva to Vice-Admiral Drake."

"Go ahead, Linsey."

"I've found a possible answer to the alternate food source problem for you."

"Do tell," replied Amanda, excitement clear in her voice.

"At one time the Igen carried food animals, livestock. They depended on this as part of their food source, but when the war started the Growes cut off the Gants' supply of meat. The Gants retained access to plant food, and still do, but it's been a long time since they had any other source of meat except Growes.

"They became cannibals out of a need to survive. I'm betting some of those animals might still exist in that forest the Admiral wanted to explore."

"This is great news, Linsey. Good work. I'll contact Floo and see what he has to say about this."

A New Alliance

"Rayla, what's going on? You're being quieter than me. It's disturbing."

She smiled wryly and patted Twelve's hand as she replied. "Retriever is shipping out with Orca for the refuel and supply run. Looks like we'll be gone for about two weeks. I don't want to be away from you for so long."

"I don't want that either," sighed Twelve. "Ah well, such is the nature of the life we lead. I endured solitary expulsion on Elysium many times, I can do this. Just don't forget me while you're gone."

Rayla chuckled and snuggled deeper into her embrace. "How could I ever forget my super SUVI. I will miss you like crazy though.

"Sweetheart, what did you mean, solitary expulsion on Elysium?"

"It was one of First Prime's motivators, please him and you earned extra time with other SUVI, displease him, and get sent to the surface alone during migration time for weeks. I got sent out several times."

"Is that when you became such a loner?"

"I suppose it is. Antha says I developed it as a survival strategy, staying a bit apart so it wouldn't hurt so bad when I was sent out for long periods. A hunt was usually only a couple of days, but Solitary was for much longer. You only knew when it was over because another hunter would come looking for you."

"Wow. Gods, girl, I can't even imagine a life like that. Will you be okay while I'm gone?"

"I'll miss you like crazy, but I'll be okay. There are other SUVI around, and I'll hang out with Kim, pry all your deep dark secrets out of him."

Rayla laughed at that. "He'll talk too, the rat. Keep an eye out for him?"

"You're extremely protective of him, aren't you?"

"Yeah, I am, can't help it, he's still my baby brother."

"All right, my precious girl, I'll be the big sister while you're gone."

With that assurance to comfort her Rayla settled down on Twelve's shoulder and drifted off to sleep. Next morning they lingered over breakfast then Twelve walked her to the ship. A short while later Retriever launched. "There she goes," sighed Twelve. "Might as well go find Kim."

* * * * *

While Twelve mentally adjusted to the hollow feeling in her heart, Amanda was deep in conversation with Linsey, Tonts, and Floo. She had transported the two war leaders aboard the Reacher for the meeting.

"I don't see so many Rontons with you today, Amanda."

"I trust I won't need them, Floo. Will I?"

He sighed and sank into a chair. "I hope not. You won't need them to protect you from me anyway."

"Nor me," agreed Tonts. "We should tell you, Amanda, Floo and I have been communicating with the aid of your magical comm units and the translating devices. It has been somewhat enlightening, at least for me."

"Starting to see us as more than just meat, Tonts?"

"That and a deadly enemy, yes. It is hard to see anyone or anything as more than a food source when you're facing starvation."

Floo nodded and sighed. "Yes, I can understand that. My father once convinced the people we should share the food. He believed that, if we offered to share, the Gants would stop hunting us."

"I was unaware of that attempt at reconciliation."

"It didn't happen, Tonts. The day he tried to make contact we were hit by a hunting party. My father was taken to nourish the children of the enemy. I hope they choked on the meat."

"They probably did if he was as tough as you," chuckled Tonts. "Is that when you became the leader?"

"It was."

"It was your rise to power that brought me to a leadership position."

"Oh?"

"Yes, your raids were so swift and deadly, two leaders perished in rapid succession. I became the leader and chose to run and hide rather than fight in open combat. We became stealthy hunters instead of warriors. More of us survived that way."

"I must say, it is good to see you two getting along so well," smiled Amanda.

"The need to survive forces one to adapt to unusual things," sighed Floo. "For me, I would fight on, or destroy Igen to prevent anymore Growes from nourishing the Gants. However, this isn't about me, it's about the young Growe who is just now learning to speak, the old Growe who has spent her life tending the sick, and others.

"They deserve a chance at life, a chance for a life without the fear of the hunters. If I can give them that then I can endure much, even Tonts."

Tonts chuckled at that. "At least we agree on that, Floo. It's not about us, it's about the young Gant just being born, and his children. If we can solve this, our people, our combined peoples, can spend their lives tending to Igen without fear. It's a dream worth striving for, is it not?"

"It is that," agreed Floo.

"I'm curious," smiled Amanda, "how did you contact each other, begin this delightful dialogue?"

"That's all Selea's fault," grinned Floo. "She somehow turned on her comm in her sleep. It was Keta who answered. The two women talked to each other that night, and again the next. When Selea came to me with a warning from Tonts about what was happening, I mistrusted it, but was curious.

"His warning of a raid was indeed accurate, and his enemy was somewhat unhappy to find so many armed and ready Growes waiting for him. At Eelee's insistence, I tried the comm and called Tonts; to my great surprise he answered.

"We exchanged information a few times over the next number of days, slowly building a trust between us. It's a task in progress, but we're getting there."

"The meat was a nice touch," said Tonts.

"The meat?" asked Amanda.

"Yes, there are large beasts, smaller beasts, and some things that crawl that are edible. We Growes eat them instead of Gants. We do prefer vegetation, but some meat must be eaten to prevent the sickness."

"And we Gants are happy that you do," chuckled Tonts. "As a gesture of peace between us, Floo sent us to a large cache of food. The meat had an unusual taste, but it was delicious. I will confess, that was the first time in years I went to sleep on guard duty."

That made Floo laugh, then he responded to Amanda's raised eyebrow. "The meat has something in it that makes you drowsy. We thought nothing of it because we're accustomed to it, but Eelee said I should warn Tonts anyway."

"The warning came a bit late," chuckled Tonts. "We'd already eaten the meat so I told everyone to rest, that I would remain on watch. Sadly, I was somewhat less than watchful.

"So, enough pleasantries, may I ask why you have brought us here, Amanda?"

"I brought you here to tell you Linsey has found information that might help us solve the alternate food source problem. Long ago on Igen, the Gants ran the ship; were the crew. Floo's people were called Growers then. They tended the crops and animals, controlled the food for all. At that time some of those animals were used for a food source.

"Our people rarely if ever eat the meat of an animal, but our greatest healer has told me that won't work for you, at least not with the plants you have available on Igen."

"How does he know what plants are on Igen?"

"I helped him gather samples, Tonts," said Floo. "The great leader brought a woman over and she took samples of every plant she could find. She took them back to the great healer to study, that and a sample of my blood."

"Your blood? How ... Oh, the supreme leader was there. Did she hold you down and take the blood?"

Floo chuckled at that. "She didn't have to. I'm not in favor of fighting a losing battle if I can avoid it. She explained what she wanted so I gave in. Amanda's companion scares me, Tonts, and I will admit it. I don't scare easily, but there's something about her that tells me life will be better if I don't make her angry."

"I believe you," sighed Tonts. "We have fought many battles over the years, Floo. Your courage has never been in question.

"So, Amanda, you believe the meat of these animals to be the answer to the food problem?"

"Yes, I believe it could be. The original builders of Igen put them aboard as a food source, and many generations followed, so the food must be adequate for good health. I'd like to get a sample for Dr. Reilly to test."

"Allow me," said Floo. "Floo to Selea."

"Here Floo. What do you need?"

"Is there any meat left from last night's feast?"

"A few scraps only."

"That would be sufficient," he replied as he saw Amanda nodding her head. "Hold some in your hand; Amanda will arrange for you to join us."

Even as he spoke, Amanda was on her comm, talking to Transport. Selea arrived with a sample of the meat and Amanda contacted Dr. Reilly who came immediately. They soon had their answer.

"Reilly to Amanda."

"Here."

"That's it, the missing enzyme is there. I'll bet all living creatures on that ship carry it, but not the plants."

"Thank you, Dr. Reilly. Amanda out. Well, there we have it, gentlemen, the answer to the problem. The rest is in your hands. What will you do?"

"I'll be happy to have my people hunt beasts instead of Gants, as long as they're safe to do so. I'm tired of all the killing. The older I get the more I like my father's plan."

"I agree, Floo; I too tire of the killing. The big problem before us now is Jara. That man has more followers than I at the moment, and he is determined to kill every Growe alive, kill them or confine them to breeding pens to use for food. He especially enjoys the meat of the young.

"I see your anger, Floo, and I agree. Yes, we could join forces and wipe them out, but far too many would die on both sides. Igen is vast, and we Gants and Growes are too few. If we are to properly care for her, our Igen, we must stop killing each other."

Floo relaxed back and sighed. "I can't argue with that. So, what's the plan; how do we get you back in control of all Gants?"

"We're working on that," replied Tonts. "We've left Jara in control of the many, but he struggles to feed them. Since you and I have been coordinating our efforts they've had no meat, nor have his fighters. Eventually they will weaken, and we can step in to take over."

"What will you do with Jara?"

"Kill him. He has tried to kill me in my sleep several times, and he has put unwelcome hands on Keta. Jara will die and I will rule. When that day comes, Floo, your people will be left in peace to hunt."

"What of the others, Tonts, the young and the old, the infirm and more, will they not all perish before Jara's fighters weaken?" asked Amanda.

"That's true, Amanda, but I have a plan. I'll need your help, Floo, if my plan is to work."

"I'm listening."

"My plan is to start sneaking small rations of meat to the weaker members of our people. This will be extremely dangerous, for if we're caught, Jara will kill the lot of us."

"You need me to supply the meat."

"In a word, yes."

Floo looked thoughtful then nodded. "It could be done, Tonts, but renks are hard to find and harder to kill. We often eat other beasts and crawlers, but the meat of the renks is by far the best. The problem is, your enemy is getting desperate, his patrols are ever on the hunt and it's taking most of my fighters to counteract him, keep safe our elders and young."

"I may have an answer for you there, Floo," grinned Amanda. "My companion was once a mighty hunter, and so was Twelve, the one you fought. I'll bet they would be willing to do the hunting for you."

"Are you serious?"

"I am. Shall I ask her for you?"

"By all means, Amanda."

"Amanda to Admiral Sorenson."

"Here, Mandy."

"I've got Floo and Tonts here in my office. They need a couple of volunteer hunters to provide meat."

"Hunters?"

"The forests of Igen contain fierce beasts that they hunt for food. Floo and Tonts have concocted a plan that requires more meat than Floo can spare the hunters to gather. If we can find a few hunters to provide the meat, Floo can focus his fighters on protecting his people from the rebel Gants."

Amanda grinned at Jeannie's instant response. "I'll go myself."

"You might want to take Twelve with you. You did say she wanted to go hunting there, and by your own order, no SUVI is allowed on Igen alone."

"Capital idea, Vice-Admiral. I'll find Twelve then come to your office."

"We'll be here," grinned Amanda.

"Only two hunters? The renks are large and fierce beasts."

"Floo, let me tell you about the first time I met my companion," smiled Amanda. "I was working at Transportation ..."

Amanda was just finishing her story when Jeannie and Twelve arrived wearing hunting leathers, carrying huge knives and short spears. "Someone called for hunters?"

"Yes we did, Admiral," grinned Amanda.

She outlined the basic plan for Jeannie who nodded approvingly. Jeannie turned to Floo and spoke. "If this is a plan to capture me, know I have left instruction with the captain of the Reacher to punch a hole in Igen's side, to let the ship bleed atmosphere until all within are dead and then destroy it if I do not return.

"One of Igen's people has already taken and harmed some of our people, but we took them back. This ..."

"Peace, Great Leader," said Tonts, holding up his hands. "That fool was the rebel, Jara, and our plan is to feed my people, protect Floo's people, protect your folk, while we locate and kill Jara. In this way we hope to bring peace to Igen. The meat is the key to the success of this plan, without it we have no hope."

Jeannie gazed into his eyes for a long moment then nodded. "Accepted. Floo, permission to hunt in your forest?"

"Granted with honor, Great Leader. I only regret I can't go with you, but Jara is getting desperate and attacking everywhere. I should be getting back to my people."

"Then let's go," grinned Jeannie, "Twelve is getting restless for the hunt." Twelve chuckled at that as they led the way back to Transportation.

Hunting

Missing your girlfriend, Rayla?" grinned SUVI 20.

"Huh? Oh, yeah, I am actually. This mission is boring as hell, and I have nothing else to do except miss Twelve. How do you do it, Twenty? You're the only SUVI on the ship, but you seem to be okay all the time."

"It's odd really, but it's the Captain. Sessas and I bonded under unique conditions, and she's more like a SUVI than anything else. Having Sessas near is like having another SUVI with me and it keeps me grounded.

"I'll admit it's weird, this being an alien and all. Back when I was a human I was always content in my own company, but as a SUVI I do need part of my herd near to keep me sane."

Rayla chuckled at that. "Back when you were a human, Twenty, you have no idea just how crazy that sounds."

"Yeah, but it's true. I can remember it, being human, but it's like it was somebody else, like a character in a book I've read or something. I can't really connect to it and all.

"Rayla, I'm getting strong impressions from you, and I think I might know why."

"Stay out of my head, Twenty."

"Sorry, when I was human I could always mind my own business, but as a SUVI I just can't seem to do it."

"Well try harder," chuckled Rayla.

"Okay, if I have to. Rayla, just keep in mind what slavery must have been like for them and be patient. Her nature will overcome her instinctive fears in time. She'll get there if you're patient."

"Thanks, Twenty. Patience has never been my strong suit; guess I'd better start working on that."

"Good idea. Look, it's boring as sin here. The ship is just sitting on the ground watching the salvage crews hunt and gather. Here's my war hammer, go out and beat the snot out of a few rocks and trees, take your mind off your troubles."

Rayla grinned as she accepted the long-handled hammer and rose to her feet. "Dang fine idea, Twenty. Thanks." She stepped outside and ran at a tree screaming her battle cry.

Captain Sessas stepped in behind SUVI 20. "Rayla need distraction?"

"That she did."

"Was good choice, Sister Tentee. She feel better after good fight with tree." Twenty smiled at her friend's hissing laughter.

* * * * *

While Rayla went to war with a tree, and Suvi-jean went hunting with SUVI 12, Jara the rebel got news he didn't like. "Nothing?"

"Nothing, Jara. They're being watchful, and fearful. Before, when they'd fight we would have a chance, but now they hide deep in the forest where they know the pathways. If we chase them in there, we get ambushed. We lost three but have no meat to show for it. Our Rontons grow weak as do the elders and young."

Jara didn't respond until prompted. "Jara? What do you want us to do?"

"Go hunting, don't come back without meat. They're Growes, inferior, weaker, use your heads and lure them out where you can get at them. Set fire to the forest if you have to."

Shocked, the man pulled back from him. "You would burn Igen?"

"No," sighed Jara as his shoulders drooped. "I'm just getting desperate. We need food, the elders and young need food. Damn that fool Tonts anyway, he should be here helping us. Instead he fights us, forcing us to divide our troops. How are we supposed to provide for our people like this?"

He sat in thought for several moments and no one disturbed him.
Suddenly he rose to his feet. "Everybody able to hold a spear come with
me. I've had enough of this."

"Jara, where are we going?"

"To get meat for our people."

"But ..."

"The outsiders. We know where to find them. They taste foul, but
at least it'll be meat." He grabbed up his spear and, followed closely by
his Ronton and then the others, headed out for Growe territory.

The three security people outside the door to Igen's bridge got a
call. "Reacher to Security Sub-commander Glenn."

"Here."

"There's a large number of aliens moving in your direction. You
could have incoming."

"Understood. How many?"

"Dozens. Get the engineers out."

"Copy that."

"Do you need additional forces?"

"Unknown at this time. Stand by for transporting engineers."

Moira Duncan and her people were quickly transported back to
the Reacher. A few moments later Hal White and a number of
additional troops arrived. "This one's your show, Kar, where do you
want us?"

"Inside, sir. If they get past us they're all yours."

"Understood."

It took a while for the Gant forces to reach them, but they did.
"Here they come."

Jara was first to arrive with his followers close behind. "They're just
standing there, waiting to nourish." He waved his spear in the air and
charged at the three people guarding the door. "Today we gather meat
and retake the room of full control."

One woman stepped toward the swiftly advancing Gants and raised some sort of weapon. Jara hurled his spear with all his strength, but it bounced off the outsider, barely causing her to take a step back. In the next moment the outsider fired her weapon. Jara and those closest to him were hurled back, tumbling into those behind them.

All was in chaos as the thrown spear had no effect, but the strange weapons were like facing an unrelenting hand as it hurled them back time and time again. After being tossed through the air a third time, Jara turned and retreated, his fighters close behind him.

Battered and exhausted, they weren't ready for the ambush as a dozen Growes stepped around a corner and threw their spears then fled into the trees nearby.

It was late and the lights were dimming as they reached their sanctuary once again. "Did we lose any?" asked Jara as he sank to the floor, exhausted.

"Only two, Sen Jara," replied his personal Ronton. "It was the spears of the Growes. The outsiders threw us away but made no kills. The Growes killed two, but fled into the trees where we dare not follow."

At that point Jara noticed an old woman chewing contentedly. He rose and went to her. "What are you eating?"

"The last of the food I was given," she replied.

"Given? Who gave you food?"

"Tonts. He and Keta brought food for all. Not much, but enough to fill a belly. He said you could find your own."

In a rage, Jara struck and the woman was dead. That act was enough, several of his fighters slipped away in the night. They sought out the places they thought Tonts might be hiding. Eventually, near the coming of new light, they were found.

"Drop all weapons," commanded Tonts as he and several fighters appeared with drawn spears. They obeyed and sank to the floor. "Is this all of you?"

"It is, Sen Tonts."

"Why are you here?"

"We have left Jara to his fate," sighed one. "I agree that we need meat, and Jara promised meat, Growes in the breeding pens, meat for all."

"But?"

"It didn't happen, Sen Tonts. The Growes have fled into the forests, all of them. We hunt, but with only veg for food, and little enough of that, we grow weak. There is no meat to be had and we're dying, all of us.

"Jara led us against the outsiders seeking a different source of meat, but we were defeated then attacked by Growes. When we finally returned to find you had given food to the elders, Jara flew into a rage and killed the old woman who told him. He's completely mad, Sen Tonts, and no fit leader. We came seeking for you, to join your people."

"Before that happens there is much you need to know, much to consider."

"Oh? What do you mean?"

"We have a way to access food, meat as well, but we can never again hunt or eat the Growes. They are allies now; they bring us food."

"The Growes? They willingly nourish? How ...?"

"No. No, the Growes do not nourish, nor will they ever again. No, the Growes eat the meat of animals they find in the trees. You know of what I speak, for the old tales tell of a time when animals were the source of meat for all. This is how the Growes stay strong without eating the bodies of fallen Gants."

"How can you know this, Sen Tonts?"

"I have spoken often with their leader. We both agree that there's been enough killing, enough war. We ..."

At that point Keta came trotting up with her Ronton. "They're alone, Tonts; they weren't followed."

"Good to know."

"Floo to Tonts."

Tonts adjusted the comm unit and replied. "Here, Floo. What's the good word?"

"The hunters are in the forest, Tonts. I expect there will be meat for all very soon."

"Good news indeed, Floo. May Igen nurture you this day." Tonts let his arm fall away from his shoulder and sighed. "There you have it, people. The Growes will soon provide us with meat, and we will do all we can to see they are left alone to do it."

"Tonts?"

"You came to us asking to join us. This is who we are, this is what we do. We are allies of the Growes; we will protect them as best we can. We will also do what we can to provide food for our own elders and young. Jara and his followers can starve for all I care.

"So, to join us, this is the price you pay. You must swear to never again hunt, kill, or eat, a Growe. You will help me defend them and all the peoples of Igen, Gant and Growe alike. Jara is the enemy here, and he must be stopped."

"Agreed," sighed one of the men. "If the Growes are willing to give me food I will gladly stand back and let them hunt." The rest agreed.

* * * * *

Amanda and Rhonda were in Simple Pleasures enjoying a taste of Alli's latest invention when they got the report. "Commander White to Vice-Admiral Drake."

"Here Hal. Everything under control?"

"Clear here. We were hit by a large number of Gants, but the armor did the job and Kar taught them the effects of a scatter blaster. It worked well and they fled. I'd say it's safe for Moira and company to return."

"Good news indeed, Hal. Thank you." Amanda smiled and nodded to Rhonda who reached for her own comm.

"Captain Moore to Chief Engineer."

"Moira here."

"Hal says the war's over, you can go back to work now."

"Music to my ears. Thank you captain." Within moments they were back on Igen's bridge.

* * * * *

Later that day on Igen, Moira Duncan sighed and straightened up, stretching the kinks out of her back. "Well, that's about it for the bridge, at least from an Engineering standpoint. The next step is getting to main Engineering and fix that damned reactor so we can get the engines back online."

"That's not going to be any fun," sighed Hal. He was half asleep in the captain's chair. "That place is hot with radiation and deep in Gant territory. They're still in the throes of a civil war."

"Dammit, this whole thing is taking way too long."

"Yeah, second that. Anyway, not my call. I'll let you and Mandy figure out when to go, then I'll have my people ready."

"You're right there, not our call. Still, I'm willing to admit, hanging around here in interstellar space is giving me the creeps. I'll be more than happy to see that boring star system up ahead."

"Amen to that, Commander, amen to that."

* * * * *

While the Reacher's security forces were fending off an attack by the Gant rebels, two hunters slipped into the forest that had once been carefully cultivated gardens. Jeannie took a long deep breath and smiled with delight. "I have to confess, Twelve, I do miss the chance to go hunting once in a while."

"Agreed," chuckled SUVI 12. "So, do we do this like the old days, enjoy the forest for a few days then hunt like we mean it?"

Jeannie laughed at that. "Tempting, isn't it? Let's go see what we can find then decide."

"Works for me. You lead and I'll keep an eye out for nasty surprises."

"We have a plan," said Jeannie as she set out slowly, scanning all around carefully. This wasn't the more open plains like Elysium, this was dense forest. All her senses, her intuition, were on full alert, and her eyes glowed amber. She grinned as she saw Twelve sniffing the air, listening intently, searching for a new scent, a sound that didn't belong.

The lights of Igen began to dim and they stopped for a ration bar and a sip of the water they'd brought with them. "What's on your mind, Twelve."

"Got a bit distracted, did I?"

"No, you've been as alert as ever, but I can hear your gears turning."

"You intuitives make me crazy," chuckled Twelve. "Alright. I guess I'm wondering how you did it Five. How did you get past the instinct to fight or freeze up every time she tried to touch you? I know you have, it's easy to see."

"I feel your pain, my sister," sighed Jeannie. "I was terrified at first, afraid of being hurt, afraid I'd lose control and hurt her. I told her early on, no sex."

Twelve chuckled at that. "Yeah, how did that work out?"

"As you've already guessed, she was having none of that. It took her a while, but she slowly, gently, worked her way past my fears. I truly do understand your problem, but I don't really know how to help you. Eighteen might have some useful insights."

"She didn't really. The thing is, I'm so different from Eighteen, and Rayla is definitely different from Linsey. You and I are more alike, and Amanda seems to be a mix of Linsey and Rayla, ... I just wondered ..."

Jeannie put her arms around Twelve and held her gently, as they had often done for each other as young hunters on Elysium. "Think of it as just another hunt, Twelve, a different prey, a difficult track to follow, but the possible reward at the end will be worth it."

"Now you're making sense," chuckled Twelve as she returned the gentle hug. "You sleep first, I'll watch."

Jeannie nodded then settled down. A few hours later she was awakened by a hand gently shaking her shoulder. "What? Where?" Twelve pointed then moved off, Jeannie close behind.

Through the denseness of the trees they could make out a small clearing. There stood a huge beast, pawing at the ground and digging with the horn growing out of its snout. "About the size of a small Garog," mused Twelve. "That horn could be trouble, and that club on the end of its tail will bear watching."

"Indeed it will," agreed Jeannie. "I'll draw its attention; you throw the spear." She started to circle the beast through the trees, but its head came up and it snorted a challenge. She darted out in front of it then leaped aside. As the beast turned to give chase, Twelve threw her spear. The animal had moved faster than she'd expected, the spear bounced off a rib doing little more than enraging the beast. It turned and charged in a heartbeat.

As the beast gave chase, Twelve fled, circling toward Suvi-jean. They passed near each other and Jeannie tossed her spear to Twelve then suddenly flashed close by the beast who instantly changed direction to pursue her. As it turned Twelve hurled the spear which pierced its side, slicing through heart and lungs. The animal stumbled and fell dead at Jeannie's feet.

"You're getting a bit rusty," grinned Jeannie.

"Damn, that thing was fast for a beast that size. Yeah, you're right, I've been playing with the big guns on EX4 too long. I need to get groundside more often."

"Me too, my sister. I'm out of practice, that bugger nearly had me. Let's dress the kill then find a pole to carry it out on." The lights were on and the day well under way before the two SUVI staggered out of the trees carrying the carcass on a pole between them.

Floo nearly went into shock. His people had to quarter such a beast then carry it out. Shaking his head in amazement he reached for his comm. "Floo to Tonts."

"Here Floo."

"The hunters were successful; there will be meat."

"I'm pleased to hear it, Floo."

"We'll leave the food at the same location."

* * * * *

A few days later there was another meeting in progress in Amanda's office. Floo, Tonts, Amanda, Rhonda, and Moira Duncan were there. Amanda grinned as she spoke. "So, the SUVI hunters were successful?"

"Indeed they were," chuckled Floo. "It takes eight or more Growes to kill and carry a renk. Those two did it by themselves. They brought it out then went back for another. Can we keep them? Our lives would be a lot easier that way."

Amanda laughed at that. "Sorry, Floo, but I'll want them back. So, you're happy; what about you, Tonts?"

"I'm thrilled, Amanda. My people haven't been so well fed in living memory. All that remains is to rid ourselves of Jara and we will have peace on Igen."

"Tell me about that."

"Several of his fighters have abandoned him and come to our ranks. They understand that now we must protect the Growes, not hunt them for food. Jara found out that, while he was getting a just defeat at the hands of your people, we brought food to the elders and children."

"Oh? How did he take that news?"

"He struck down the old woman who told him. That caused some of his warriors to abandon him and seek us out. More followed over the next couple of days. our numbers are growing, and he has abandoned the elders. They're now under our protection and also well fed."

"Good news indeed, gentlemen. Now for me. Our people have learned what they can from Igen's bridge, and now have only one more thing to do to repair Igen. They need to access main engineering, repair the prime reactor."

At the puzzled looks she was getting, Amanda tried again. "Main engineering, the source of Igen's power, her heart if you will. As I understand it, that place is deep in Gant territory, but our sensors tell us there are no guards there."

Tonts sighed deeply. "The Heart of Igen. All who go there sicken and die. The place is forbidden, and we defend it from the Growes."

"You kept us away to keep the meat from getting spoiled," said Floo as enlightenment reached his eyes.

"Yes, Floo, that was the reasoning. If I'd thought you knew how to heal Igen's heart I'd have let you through. Please understand, without meat this would most likely be the last generation of Gants."

"Growes as well, Tonts," sighed Floo as he let his shoulders sag. "We have become too few to defend against the Gants and hunt as well. With no further need to defend against your people, and with your folk well fed, both our peoples can recover their former numbers and devote their energies to nurturing Igen."

"Agreed, Floo," nodded Tonts.

"And that brings us one step closer to the final goal for my people," smiled Amanda.

"What is that goal, Amanda?" asked Floo.

"We want to teach your folk how to care for and maintain Igen. Linsey is working on a plan to help with that right now."

"If I may, Vice-Admiral," interrupted Moira, "we still have to repair the main reactor. That's not going to be easy."

"Can you do it, Moira."

"I'm pretty sure we can, but I want to get a look at it first."

"Okay, and that creates a problem?"

"Depends on these guys and Captain Moore."

Rhonda arched an eyebrow at her so she explained. "It's hot with radiation in there. I'll need a large force of security there to make damn sure nobody else tries to get in while we're working. Then there's the other problem, even if I repair it, these folk will never dare go near it."

"Spell it out for us, Moira. What are you saying here?" said Amanda.

"Main engineering is vital to the function of any ship. I can see where these folks have rerouted most of the functions around that issue sometime in the past, but it's a temporary fix. I'd say these folks have four or five generations left before Igen fails utterly."

That news hit them hard, but it was Floo who recovered first. "Steady, Tonts, first we take care of the present generation, then the next can solve that problem."

Tonts sighed and nodded his head. "You're right, Floo. First we preserve this generation, then worry about the uncertain future.

"Amanda, I give your people full permission to occupy the area around Igen's heart and to defend it. I will pull my fighters back to defend Floo's people from Jara. If he is fool enough to go at your folk again, do as you will with him."

Learning

The meeting broke up and the people of Igen returned home. Amanda and Rhonda were on their way to the café, Simple Pleasures, when they got the announcement. "Orca fleet returning. Repeat, Orca fleet returning. Captain to the bridge." They turned their steps toward the bridge.

"Reacher, this is the Orca, Sheila Singh commanding. Please acknowledge."

Rhonda nodded to the man on comms then spoke. "Welcome back, Orca fleet. How was your trip?"

"Boring as hell, but everybody's topped up for food and fuel."

"Good to know," chuckled Rhonda. "Stand by, Orca, Vice-Admiral Drake wants a word."

"Standing by."

"Sheila, Amanda here. I'll need to shift our operations over to your ship while the Reacher goes for a refuel and food top up."

"We're at your disposal, Vice-Admiral. I'll have Brandon make room for you. What will you need?"

"I'll need Moira to commandeer your engineering department, your security forces, and some place for Linsey to work her magic."

"I'll make it happen, Vice-Admiral. Brandon will contact you when he's ready."

"Acknowledged. Amanda out. Okay, Captain Moore, as soon as we transfer over to the Orca you can gather up the rest of the fleet and head out."

"Understood," replied Rhonda, but Amanda was already walking away, contacting her people on comms.

Amanda was still organizing the changeover when Jeannie and Twelve returned to Reacher. "There you are, how was the hunting?"

"That was the most fun I've had in ages, Mandy."

"Oh really?" asked Amanda, raising an eyebrow at her.

138

Jeannie sputtered then blushed. "Dammit Mandy, we agreed there will be no embarrassing the admiral in front of the crew. Stop teasing and call a full captain's meeting. The Orca is back, and I need to ... you've already organized everything, haven't you?"

"Pretty much. How about I take you home so you can tidy yourself and get into a fresh uniform. I can give you a full report then call the meeting for you."

Jeannie gave an elaborate sigh and winked at Twelve. "Yes dear," she said. "Take me home and tidy me up." Chuckling at the playfulness of those two, Twelve turned her steps toward her own quarters.

"So, that's where it stands right now," said Amanda as she finished bringing Jeannie up to speed.

"And you say Linsey has a plan to take things to the next level?"

"Yes. We all know that just fixing the ship won't really do much except give them a few more generations to work on the problem, but that's all. Linsey says we need to teach them to read and write in the original language so they can communicate without the translators and so they can read the manuals, learn how to make future repairs on their own."

"She's right, but we can't take the time, remain here long enough to make that happen."

"I know, but she says she has a plan."

"I can't wait to hear it," chuckled Jeannie. "Now, I have a surprise for you. Twelve and I took a day ... okay, two days, to explore a bit. We found the abandoned shuttle bay with several small ships that looked intact. Perhaps we can get those functional and train a pilot or two in case they need them in the future."

"I'll put Ebony to work on that one. She can figure out how to fly one then Edran can make a VR to train the pilots."

"I like it, Mandy. Call that meeting now; I'm sure Rhonda is anxious to get under way."

* * * * *

"Everyone's here, Admiral," said Rhonda as Jeannie and Amanda entered the briefing room.

"Thank you Captain Moore. All right, people, let's all find out where we are and proceed from there. Vice-Admiral Drake, please update everyone on the status of the Igen project."

"Of course, Admiral. In short, people, we're nearly done. We've learned as much as we can, made as many repairs as we could, and now Moira is gearing up to do what she can to repair the main reactor.

"We'll be shifting our efforts over to the Orca while Reacher leads the rest of the fleet to the next system for refuel and supply run. The Kreenon will fly as Reacher's escort for that trip.

"Our next step is to educate the citizens of Igen in the elder language of those who originally built the ship. Captain da Silva has a plan to speed up the teaching efforts with the Igen inhabitants, and the admiral herself can give us a better picture of how the food replacement system is working on Igen."

"Time for my report?" chuckled Jeannie. "Okay, SUVI 12 and I transported over to Igen to see if the idea of hunting would provide enough meat to supply the whole population. I'm happy to report it will, easily. At this moment the Gants are no longer hunting the Growes, but instead are guarding them to allow their hunters the freedom to work.

"The rebel faction is still at large, but Tonts seems to believe that will be well in hand soon enough. We brought them enough meat for several days then returned to Reacher.

"Now, while we were there, Twelve and I found what was once their shuttle bay with several small ships intact. Engineers are already on their way over to see if they're functional."

"Are we planning to confiscate those shuttles?" asked Captain Baris, Jeannie's grandfather.

"No, my conscience, we're not. However, Moira tells us the Growes and Gants have five, maybe six generations left on Igen before the main reactor fails utterly. We've got the means to make VR training module for their people to learn to pilot those shuttles, we can also help them turn Igen to a course that should see them eventually reach a possible planet."

"You'd find them a planet to colonize, but not us?" asked one of the passenger representatives.

Jeannie sighed and didn't rise to the bait. "They won't have a Reacher to nourish them, and I don't know if it will work, but it's the best chance we can give them."

"Steer them to the next system, Admiral," said Captain Morthel of the explorer, EX2. "That planet's not great, but it would give them a chance."

"What's Commander Peters say about it, Morthel?" asked Jeannie.

"Lily gave it a five," she chuckled in reply. "Far from ideal, but doable in a pinch."

"Then that will be the plan we take to them," smiled Jeannie. "Now, my curiosity is getting the better of me, Captain da Silva. Care to share this plan of yours with us?"

"Of course, Admiral. As you know, my ship, Friendship, went with the Orca fleet to refuel in the next system, but I was able to talk to your fighter ship. He agrees it can be done.

"The plan is to use the teaching technology of those two ships, Friendship and F1, to teach a few of the Growes and Gants the elder language of Igen's builders. Once they have that they can talk to each other without the translators, plus they can read the old manuals, make their own repairs in future, perhaps even make improvements. Those chosen few can then proceed to teach the rest of their combined peoples these skills as we don't have the time to spend on that."

"What kind of time are we looking at, Linsey?"

"F1 says it will take a full day to teach both spoken language and written. He has already absorbed the required knowledge, and I have Friendship working on it now."

"It's Amanda's project, Linsey, but I like it. It makes sense to me."

"And to me as well," smiled Amanda. "Do it Linsey, make it happen."

"Okay, that's it from here. Sheila, report. Tell us of the grand adventure in the next system."

"Aye, Admiral. Well, it was boring as can be. Two planets worth a look, one in the zone sporting lots of ruins, but nothing of great value on either. We topped up our fuel, Lilly Peters loaded our poor ships with crate after crate of samples, Rayla Milla used SUVI 20's war hammer to beat the crap out of a tree, then we came home. End report."

Everybody was laughing at that. "How did Rayla get her hands on the warmaiden?" asked Jeannie.

"Tentee give," chuckled Sessas. "Rayla bored, give hammer, declare tree enemy. Stress relief."

"Wish I could have seen that," smiled Jeannie. "Okay, Mandy, move your operations over to Orca so Rhonda can go for refuel. Ka'Ron, you're flying security for Reacher on this one. I'll send Nine with F1 for his refuel. Linsey can put him to work when you get back.

"Is there anything further? No? Then the meeting is adjourned."

What to do Next

While Suvi-jean went for her change of clothes and report from Amanda, SUVI 12 ran to her own quarters, hoping to find Rayla there. She wasn't, but she wasn't far behind. She burst through the door and flew into Twelve's arms, whispering her name over and over."

"Hush now, precious girl, hush. I've got you," breathed Twelve as she hugged Rayla tightly. They had only a moment before the comms pinged.

"All EX4 crew, pack up. We're shipping out for a refit. Repeat, all EX4 crew, pack up and report to the ship."

"Ah crap," sighed Twelve. Suddenly Rayla kissed her fully on the lips. Twelve fought herself to be still and allow it, then she slowly began to like it and respond.

"Oh my god, Twelve, I'm so sorry," said Rayla as she suddenly realized what she'd done and tried to get out of Twelve's arms.

Twelve held her fast. "Don't be sorry, my girl. I survived, and I think I liked it. Hold that thought until I get back then we'll revisit the idea." With that she reluctantly released Rayla from her embrace.

"Twelve, did I hear that right?"

"Yes you did, but you can't do it again, not now. If you do I'll probably mutiny and miss the ship, the admiral will beat me up and ..."

"I'll help you pack; I'll miss you like crazy until you get back, but I'll be fine as long as I can look forward to that conversation."

"You can, and so will I," sighed Twelve as she turned and began packing a couple of fresh uniforms into her knapsack.

Rayla walked her to the ship then gave her a bone-cracking hug before releasing her. "Give her up, Rayla," chuckled Hal. "I need my gunners. You can have her back when we return in a few days." Blushing furiously, Rayla released her grip on Twelve and backed away. She stood watching as the hatch closed then EX4 launched. EX4 was already in space when Jeannie adjourned the meeting.

* * * * *

"What is it, Tonts?"

"Keta, my love, we may have a problem."

"Oh?"

"Yes. Another five fighters have left Jara's group and joined with us."

"And that's bad because?"

"I don't trust them; they were always among his close companions. I fear we may have spies among us, or worse. If he suddenly attacks, I don't want to be skewered from behind by a traitor. Speak quietly to those you trust, have them watch our new recruits carefully." She nodded and trotted away, speaking softly to her Ronton.

Tonts looked around to be sure he was alone then reached for his comm and called. "Tonts to Floo."

"Here Tonts."

"Floo, another five of Jara's fighters have joined my ranks, but I have a bad feeling here. We'll watch them closely for treachery but keep a sharp eye out anyway."

"Understood. Thanks for the warning."

Floo looked thoughtful for a moment then noticed Selea trying to get his attention. He motioned her forward. "What is it, my sister?"

"I just had a call from Keta."

"Did she warn you about the possible traitors in their ranks?"

"She did, yes. You already knew?"

"Tonts told me the same. We'll keep sharp eyes on the paths just in case."

"I've also heard from Linsey. She wants me to be the first to test the learning of the elder speech. Should I go?"

"Go, Selea, learn what you can. Everything we can learn will be a help to us in the future."

* * * * *

Selea tentatively settled the cap of wires and more on her head then reeled as a barrage of sounds and symbols assaulted her senses. Hours later it slowed then stopped. She had only moments to catch her breath then the voice of the machine showed her a picture and demanded the name of the symbol. That continued for another hour then the machine went silent.

Slowly, Selea shook off the spell and turned to find Linsey nearly asleep in the captain's chair. She rose then took the translator from Selea's collar. Linsey smiled as she stepped back and spoke. <So, did it work? Can you understand me?>

<Of course. How can you speak this language?>

<I tested the learning module yesterday,> grinned Linsey as she pinned the translator back on Selea's collar. "Okay, now look at this tablet and tell me what it says."

Selea looked at the display of symbols then a smile of delight spread across her face. "It says, personal log, first officer of Igen. It was exciting as we set sail today, heading into the unknown. Linsey, wouldn't this have been recorded in voice?"

"It was, but the ship translated it to text for teaching purposes. Now, you have to practice the language and reading every day so you don't lose it."

"I understand, Linsey, but who do I speak it with?"

<Me,> said a voice. Selea turned to see a Gant woman smiling at her. <At last we meet in person, Selea. I'm Keta.>

Selea smiled with delight and held out her hand. <We meet in joy, Keta. I'll call every day.>

<It is my hope that soon we will be able to meet in person as friends aboard Igen.>

<I will look forward to that day, friend Keta.>

"All right, girls, save it for later. I need to get you both back to your people then I need ten hours of sleep," said Linsey. She guided them to the transport pad then Eighteen threw the switch to send them home to Igen.

* * * * *

Jara stood with his back pressed tightly to the wall, waiting. A man slipped around the corner to join him. "We must be swift, Jara. They watch us carefully."

"Have you had any luck?"

"None, Tonts never seems to sleep and his Ronton the same. However, I have learned where they get the food."

"Tell me."

"From the Growes."

"What? The Growes willingly nourish?"

"No, Jara. There are creatures that live in the forests. The Growes hunt them for meat. Tonts has made an alliance with the Growes. We guard their territory while they hunt for meat and gather vegetation. Tonts protects his new allies, and they give us food. Never in my life have I been so well fed."

"So, you've become a servant of the Growes like Tonts?"

"No, Jara, but I do grow strong again."

"You must learn where they hunt these creatures. We can hunt for our own food, and when we recover our strength we will kill Tonts and take full control of Igen. Go back now, learn what you can. Return in two days, I'll be waiting."

The man nodded then peeked around the corner before disappearing. Jara went the other way. Neither man had seen the small face peering out at them from the air duct overhead. When she was certain they were gone the small girl child slid the grate aside and dropped easily to the floor then fled to find Keta.

Keta approached Tonts with a child in tow. "Ah, there you are. How did the learning with Linsey go?"

"Perfect. I learned the elder language as did Selea of the Growes. We spoke together in that language. Now, my young friend here has a secret to tell you. Go ahead Tili, whisper in his ear, tell him what you told me."

The child approached Tonts then spoke softly as she related what she'd heard the two men talking about. He gave no outward sign, but a cold rage was building up in his heart. When she finished he gave her a pat on the shoulder and a piece of the meat from his portion. She walked away chewing contentedly. "What should we do, Tonts?"

"Call your friend, Selea. Use the elder language, relate to her what we've learned. Floo can keep an eye out for would-be hunters that don't belong. We'll watch as well."

Keta nodded and reached for her shoulder pin, covering the translator with her hand. <Keta to Selea.>

<Selea here.>

<Selea, listen to this ...>

She listened carefully then nodded. <Thank you, friend Keta. I will inform Floo at once.>

"It's done, Tonts."

"Good. I now leave you in charge here. Floo and I are to get the teachings today." He reached for his comm. "Tonts to Linsey. Ready."

* * * * *

While Linsey educated those who had first received the comms and the leaders of the two factions, Moira Duncan and the engineers from Orca worked carefully in full radiation suits. A half hour of work then six hours of rest in a special shielded room aboard Orca. First they were hosed down to remove any contamination then they stripped off the suits and went to rest.

They were resting on the benches when a voice came over the speaker. "Looks like you're all clear, Commander Duncan. There are no signs of anything on instruments; come on out and have a bite to eat. Grateful, they left the small waiting room to find a makeshift cafeteria waiting for them. The captain's personal chef grinned with delight as they dug in.

"You look familiar," Moira said to the chef as she returned for seconds of dessert. "Where do I know you from?"

"I was in charge of Sanitation aboard the Reacher for years," sighed the chef. "I was there so long I damn near forgot how to cook."

Moira chuckled at that. "I'd say your memory is pretty good, my friend." Just then Amanda arrived with Captain Singh.

"Moira, how's it going?"

"Well, we didn't have enough time for more than a look, but I believe we can stabilize the reactor and get those engines started. Sheila, I'd recommend you rotate your security people out every three hours. They're nowhere near the worst of the radiation, but better to be safe than sorry."

"Will do, Moira, and thanks."

Moira turned back to Amanda. "I'll give the builders their due, they built a ton of shielding into main engineering in case of just this happening. If all had gone as they originally planned this reactor would still be ticking along perfectly."

"Gone as planned?"

"Succeeding generations as enthusiastic about the mission as the original crew," sighed Moira.

"Yeah, that would have been a big help to them. I'm glad our folk managed to invent the star drive before we got caught up in the same situation."

"Second that," sighed Moira.

"So, any idea of a timeline to repairs?"

"I don't want to be in there any longer than a half hour at a time, Amanda. That's going to slow us down a bunch. I'd say we should be getting finished up by the time Reacher gets back if all goes well."

"Good to know. I'll let Linsey know she's got a few more days to go."

"Linsey?"

"She's educating the Growes and Gants to the elder language, both vocal and written. She talks to them all before choosing who to educate. First she chose the leaders, then found a couple who sounded like they might make pilots."

"I don't suppose she could hunt up an engineer or two?"

Amanda chuckled at that. "Let's ask her. Amanda to Linsey."

"Here Vice-Admiral."

How's it going over there?"

"We've got the leaders working in Elder now and two who showed an interest in learning to be pilots. Right now I'm looking for possible engineers. I have one volunteer from the Gants in the learning harness right now. Still looking for a possible Growe."

"That's great work, Linsey. I'll leave you to it. Amanda out. Well there you go, Moira; she's on it."

"It's funny you know. When I first met her I truly doubted we could ever make a good engineer out of her, her heart really wasn't in it. Jeannie came along and promoted her then gave her a completely different job; now I can't imagine how we ever could have gotten this far or even survived without her."

Again Amanda smiled and agreed. "She's a real force of nature when she gets going all right. Okay, so you're all good here?"

"All good here, Vice-Admiral. We'll rest for a few more hours then go back in again and get started."

"Then I'll leave you to it. Sheila, you still have Security forces over there?"

"Yes, Ma'am, we do. Moira doesn't want any of the locals to go snooping around and make things worse. We'll rotate them out every two hours."

"All right then, I'll go abuse your transporter, get Floo and Tonts over here to bring them up to speed."

"This place is different," mused Tonts as he and Floo arrived almost simultaneously.

"Yes," replied Amanda, "this is a different ship, the Orca. You have yet to meet her captain."

"I see you have a new Ronton as well."

"Yes, Floo. Please understand, I view you, both of you, as friends and have no fear of you nor do I fear you might try to harm me. However, my companion is ever wary and so when she is off hunting on Igen, another like her will always accompany me. My companion is the greatest hunter of the SUVI, this man is the strongest of them all."

Nineteen chuckled as Floo took his measure. "Twelve, the one you fought on Igen, has told me of your speed and ferocity," smiled Nineteen. "I wanted to meet you."

"And to keep an eye on me?"

"That too," he chuckled, "but Five, our leader says you're friends now. I'm just here to meet new friends."

"And to keep an eye on us," said Floo. "Your leader is a careful hunter; I like that. So, Amanda, you called for us?"

"I did, Floo. I want to let you know where we are in the plan. Moira says that she should have Igen's heart stabilized in a few days. This will return many functions to Igen; you will have to study the manuals carefully before proceeding with anything new. Also, check the logs to make yourselves aware of any changes your ancestors may have made to the originals."

"With Tonts' help I've been able to access some of those logs. It is quite fascinating to be able to look at the thoughts and fears of our ancestors. Tell me, will Linsey continue to educate more of our people?"

"Yes, she ..."

"Ebony to Vice-Admiral Drake."

"Amanda here, Ebony, tell me good things."

"The guys here tell me six of those shuttles will be functional with a bit of tinkering. The controls appear to be pretty basic. Shouldn't take much to train a pilot, I just need to get one out into space and fly it while being filmed."

"Make it happen, Ebony."

"On it. Ebony out."

Amanda returned her attention to her guests. "My companion found several small shuttle craft aboard Igen while she was on the hunt. They appear to be functional, and that brings me to the next phase of the plan.

"As you already know, Igen's heart will not last forever. However, the Reacher and a few of our small ships are now in another star system refueling and gathering food. I've been assured your people could survive on one of the planets there. It wouldn't be easy, but it could be done.

"Now, here's what we'd like to do. As soon as Igen is ready, we'd like to change her course to take you to that planet. You would never see it, but your great grandchildren might, and they could survive there. they could take all the people and animals from a dying Igen down to the planet aboard the shuttles.

"This is the best chance for the long term survival of all your peoples. Think about it, if you like the idea we can make it happen for you. If you would rather take another path, we will not interfere."

Tonts sighed and leaned back in his chair. "It sounds good to me, Floo. We can look after this generation, but we'll need to get the youngsters excited about the possibilities."

"Agreed," said Floo, nodding. "The problem will be to keep that enthusiasm going down through the generations, but that's not our problem. We have to learn how to work together to nurture Igen. We can only give them a path; it will be up to them to walk it or not."

"Agreed," said Tonts. "Do it, Amanda. Put us on the path; it will be up to future generations to get our people there."

"Then we have a plan," said Amanda. "Now let's get you both home to Igen; there still a lot to do there."

Tonts and Floo were barely back on Igen when they felt the ship shudder slightly then rock for a short time before stabilizing. Amanda called to inform them Igen's course had changed, and they were now headed for the nearest star system. They spent the next several moments explaining this to their people reassuring everyone that it was a good thing.

However, for Jara and the few who still followed him it was quite different. They had no idea what was happening, or what it might mean. "It's the outsiders, they're destroying Igen," snarled Jara. "Tonts has betrayed us. Somehow we must find and kill him while there's still time. See, Igen regains herself, she is still stronger than the outsiders. There is still time to act."

* * * * *

While Amanda met with the leaders of Igen and the great ship was redirected toward an uncertain future, yet a future with hope, Rayla sat aboard Retriever, head in hands. "Lonesome again?" asked a gentle voice.

"Huh? Oh, hi Twenty. Yeah, I'm missing my partner, care to lend me one of yours?"

This brought a great laugh from SUVI 20. "You just keep your hands off my lovers. What's up, Rayla?"

"It was weird, Twenty, weird but sweet and full of promise. I've been trying to behave with Twelve. I understand what she must have gone through on that planet, and I'm trying to keep it safe for her."

"But?"

Rayla looked up with a sloppy grin. "I think she missed me while I was gone. Before she shipped out I kissed her before I could get myself stopped."

"And?"

"And she said she liked it. She said we could discuss it when she gets back."

"Sounds promising to me; why the long face?"

"I'm scared to death I'll mess this up. I've got a chance here, one big chance. I dare not mess it up."

"Yeah, I get that."

"So, any useful suggestions?"

Twenty's eyes twinkled with merriment. "A few," she grinned.

"Yeah? So talk already, what do I do here? How do I get her past the fear and ... Stop laughing at me, dammit."

Twenty sat beside Rayla and put her arm around the girl's shoulders, giving her a gentle hug. "Okay, I'll talk. First, if Twelve said she wants to revisit the kiss, then she truly does. I got hit with the SUVI mating drive while on that planet with Jake, learned the hard way the SUVI instinctively choose a mate and the drive to be with that person is powerful in the extreme.

"Twelve has chosen you, she'll do everything in her power to make it work between you. That mating drive will buy you a lot of forgiveness."

"Yeah, I sort of got that, but that's not how I want this to be."

"Okay, how do you want it to be?"

"Good for her all the way, no scary crap, no forcing herself to be still for me, having to force herself to tolerate my touch. How do I do that, Twenty?"

"God, this is so strange."

"What is?"

"Seeing you scared shitless," chuckled Twenty.

Rayla leaned away and punched Twenty on the shoulder. "Stop it, you fool. Help me here."

"All right. Look, this isn't as hard as you think. Who is Twelve, really?"

"What??? Wait. Okay, She's SUVI, she wants this as bad or more than I do, but her past is messing us up."

"Maybe I should have said what is Twelve?"

"What is she? Wait, she's a SUVI hunter. How does that help me?"

"You've given her a taste of something new, something she liked and wants more of. Give her more, but when she flinches become the prey, make her track you down and capture you."

"Give her complete control of the situation then tease the heck out of her to make her want more. Wow, that just might work. Thanks Twenty. I'll ..."

"All Retriever crew to the ship. Repeat, all Retriever crew to the ship."

"That was Kumar," said Twenty as she rose to her feet. "Looks like we've got a job somewhere."

"Good. I need something useful to do."

Twenty was still chuckling as Captain Sessas appeared at the hatch. "We got a job, Sister Sessas?"

"Yesss. Ebony want to play with Igen shuttle. We ride shotgun."

The job wasn't nearly as exciting as Rayla had hoped and they spent a couple of hours watching Ebony Graves make a shuttlecraft do things it was never designed to do. At the end of shift she returned to the quarters she had shared with her brother. He looked up as she entered.

"Ray, there you are. I was getting worried about you," he said as he rose and went to her.

She smiled and pulled him into a gentle hug for a moment. "Don't worry about me, little brother. I'm just bored and waiting for Twelve to get back."

"Honest?"

"Honest. It's all good."

"If you say so."

"Okay, I'm a bit on edge, but it's a good thing, not a bad thing. I'll spend a few more days training my butt off then Twelve will get home and I'll be fine again. Relax mother hen." She patted his shoulder then went to her room and prepared for bed.

Far away on another planet, SUVI 12 sat staring at the stars. Two came along and sat beside her. "Thinking about a blue eyed girl instead of the blue sky?"

"That I am, brother."

"Trying to figure out how to get past the old reactions."

"Yup, that. Any useful suggestions?"

"None worth considering, Twelve."

"Come on, you've got something on your mind or you wouldn't have spoken."

"Okay, you're holding back, but that's the reactions of a child in a pain collar. There's no collar on you now, and you have a willing mate waiting back on the Reacher. Stop being the prey and be the hunter."

"So, I should just go back and jump her bones?"

"Well, you might be a little more stealthy about it, but that's the basics," he chuckled. "You know, wait until she least expects it, then, you know ..."

"Oh shut the hell up, Two." She punched him hard on the shoulder, but he just laughed. She matched his grin then punched him again gently. "Thanks for cheering me up, Two."

"All my pleasure. So, you want the night shift?"

"All right, I'll take night guard, you big baby. Go get some sleep."

"Thanks, girl," he said as he rose to his feet, gently squeezed her shoulder then went back into the ship and to his bunk.

"Be the hunter," she snorted, "just grab her and take what I want. Damn fool, that's what they did to us. No, I'm thinking I'll talk to Rayla, tell her I need this as badly as she does, but I'm too scared to do it. She'll have to lead all the way until I get past the old fears."

Desperate Times

While everything seemed to be going smoothly, there was a problem developing. A young hunter burst from the trees and raced to Floo. "What is it? What has happened?"

"We were ambushed by Gants, three dead, Eelee was taken. Floo, they took the bodies, may they choke on the meat."

"Eelee was taken alive?"

"Yes."

"Then there's still a chance to get her back. Show me the place this happened." The young hunter set out and Floo led several others as they followed behind."

<Selea to Keta.>

<Keta here. You sound angry, Selea.>

<I am, Keta, we all are. One of our hunting parties was ambushed by Gants, three are dead and Floo's mate was taken. They took the bodies of the dead; did you know about this?>

<"I didn't, Selea. It must have been Jara. No one else would dare, Tonts would kill them for it. I'll tell him at once.> With that she set out to find Tonts. She found him in the small room of controls talking with one of the outsider's engineers. She hastily relayed what Selea had told her.

"Tonts to Floo." There was no answer. "Floo, I believe you can hear me. Know this, none of my people had anything to do with what happened. However, there are men among us who may well know where to find Jara. I'll get the information for you then kill him myself."

He got a reply to that. "I believe you, Tonts. I hope my trust is not misplaced." With that the comms went silent.

Tonts turned to Keta. "Bring me the child who overheard Jara talking to the spy in our midst." She nodded and trotted away, but soon returned with the child.

Tonts whispered to the child who nodded and started away. At Tonts' signal several fighters followed. As they neared their main camp the fighters spread out. The child reached for his hand as they walked through the people. Suddenly she pointed to one man. He hesitated for only a moment then leaped to his feet and fled.

He didn't get far before the fighters brought him down and held him fast. "Where do I find Jara?" asked Tonts as he approached. The man refused to speak. "Speak or face the consequences." The man remained silent. "Then you leave me no choice."

He rose to his feet and walked away. "Bring him."

The man was jerked to his feet and propelled along behind Tonts. "Where are you taking me?"

"To the outsiders who work at Igen's heart. They'll drag you into the hot place where your body will melt away while you suffer untold torments as Igen burns away your spirit in waves of agony."

"No!" He tried to break free, but he was held fast. Finally he stopped struggling and began to weep. "Please, Sen Tonts, not the heart of Igen, not the burning sickness. Please."

"Lead me to Jara. It's that or the heart, choose now for my patience grows thin."

Beaten, the man nodded. "He has been camping within the room of tables."

"Lead on," said Tonts as he gestured for the men to release the prisoner. "Watch him carefully. At the first sign of treachery or betrayal, kill him."

Defeated and broken, the man led off surrounded by men with spears. There was no hope for escape, the only chance he had now was to prove true and hope Tonts would relent after killing Jara.

It was a long run, but they arrived. They were cautious as they approached, but the place was empty. "They were here, Sen Tonts, I swear it."

"I believe you, for I can see signs of them everywhere and smell their scent easily. They abandoned this place not so long ago. Where would they go, do you think?"

"To the trees," sighed the man, hanging his head. "Jara was enraged when I told him you were protecting the Growes while the hunt for food for all. He must have gone there to hunt for the hunters."

"How could he manage to reach the trees without being seen?"

"Through the long tunnels."

"The long tunnels?"

"They're small and hard to get through, but we've used them before when hunting Growes. I know we were supposed to share all useful knowledge we gained on a hunt, but Jara said we needed to keep them secret in case we had a special use for them."

"Show me."

"This way."

The man led off for a short walk then stepped behind a pile of rubble and junk to move aside a panel. Tonts looked at the lettering above the panel and sighed. "Service passageways," he sighed.

"Tonts?"

"I saw reference to them in one of the manuals, Keta. They're all over Igen, passageways once used by our people to access Igen's systems to make repairs or to adjust things. I had hope to find them myself and use them to trap Jara. Now it seems the tables have turned."

Tonts jerked the prisoner forward. "Have you ever travelled this tunnel to access the trees?"

"Yes."

"Lead on. I will be right behind you with a spear at your back. Try anything foolish and I'll end your days on Igen."

"I won't, Sen Tonts, never again. I tried to tell Jara that your way was better. He didn't like hearing it."

"I'm sure he didn't. Lead on."

The hapless man led them into the twisting tunnel. It was a long time later they saw the opening ahead and the trees beyond. Jara and his few people were sitting around in a circle feasting on the bodies of the dead Growes.

Jara saw Tonts coming out of the tunnel and leaped to his feet. He threw his spear then fled into the trees. Only two of his followers managed to follow him, the rest perished to Tonts' fighters.

A lone female Growe lay struggling against her bonds as Tonts and Keta approached her. <Be still,> said Keta as she reached for the ropes that held the woman, <we won't harm you. Are you Eelee, sister of Selea?>

The woman nodded as Keta cut away the gag that was in her mouth. <Yes, I'm Eelee.> Keta nodded to Tonts who reached for his comm.

"Tonts to Floo. Jara has escaped me for the moment, but I've retrieved your companion. I also have something else of interest to show you."

<Where are you?>

<The sign overhead says Main Corridor Section Three.>

<If this is a trap ...>

<No Floo, not a trap. Speak with Eelee now.>

Tonts held the comm out for Eelee to speak. "Floo, I'm here, I'm safe. They've cut my bonds and promised not to harm me. I trust their words. Floo, by the blood of Igen."

"By the blood of Igen. Tell Tonts I'm on the way."

Eelee passed the comm back to Tonts. <He's on his way.>

<So I gathered,> chuckled Tonts. He looked up as Keta's Ronton returned, leading a number of the fighters. "Anything?"

"No, Sen Tonts. Apparently a frightened man runs much faster than an angry one. We were unable to catch him; we lost him in the trees."

"Unfortunate. Ah well, at least we managed to rescue Eelee."
<Eelee, I'm sorry we were too late to help your companions. Is there a special ceremony your people perform for your dead?>

<There is, for those we can recover. We wrap them in leaves then carry them deep into the trees where the small creatures of the forest will eventually clean the bones. We would never willingly nourish the Gants, but we are willing to nourish the forest that nourishes us.>

Tonts sighed and nodded. <I understand. Shall we help you begin to prepare these, or would you prefer we leave them for your own people to attend to?>

Eelee gazed at him for a moment then spoke. <I'd rather wait for Floo and the others. If we could lay their remains straight and beside each other that would help.>

Tonts signaled for his fighters to keep watch then bent to help Eelee arrange her dead. <There is a sight I never expected to see,> said Floo as he and several others stepped out of the trees. Eelee leaped into his arms.

"Are you all right, Eelee, truly?"

"I am Floo. These people have treated me with respect, as an equal. They rescued me from that savage who killed the others, may he choke on the meat."

"That is good news, my beloved." <Tonts, you've kept your word and proven your worth as a friend. I owe you for the return of my Eelee.>

<We're allies, Floo, there is no debt here. Shall we now hunt that accursed traitor together, or would you prefer I do it?>

<Together, Tonts. Eelee, take the others, return our hunters to the forest that nourishes us. I and one other will hunt with Tonts.>

He turned to Tonts who spoke first to Keta. "Take our fighters back to protect the people, leave these folk to mourn their dead. I'll take your Ronton with me on the hunt." <Keta, about the prisoner.>

<He will not survive the return journey.>

<Excellent. Floo, can you track those who fled this place?> Floo nodded then set out, keeping a wary eye, but moving swiftly nonetheless.

* * * * *

While Floo and Tonts hunted the last of the rebel Gants, Moira Duncan made the final adjustment and together with her team, watched the indicator needle on the gauge slowly begin to reverse direction. It all seemed anticlimactic as it returned to the safe setting.

The ancient engines hummed to life and they stepped back. "Well, lads, that appears to be it; we can do no more. Let's get out of here before we have a meltdown." She called for transport, and they soon found themselves in the decontamination area of Orca.

After they had been hosed down they stripped off and tossed the protection suits into the recycle chute, then were once again hosed down. Finally they dried off and settled down in the waiting area for the tests.

Medics in full protection suits came in and checked them over while an engineer checked to make sure there was no radiation detectable. With a sigh the small Earalithian took off his helmet and smiled. "You're all clear, friend Moira."

"Good to know, Dorind. Toss me a jumpsuit, would you?"

He passed her a fresh jumpsuit and she swiftly dressed. "I guess I should go report in now," she said as she brushed back her wet hair. "Vice-Admiral Drake will want to know what's going on." With that she stepped into new shoes and strode away.

Moira found Amanda in the office she'd been assigned, chatting with the Orca's captain. Amanda looked up as she entered. "Moira, what's the good word?"

"Success is a good one. We've stabilized the reactor, repaired as many of Igen's systems as we could. The main engines are back online, and the controls have been re-routed to the bridge. The main engine room has been sealed off for contamination. From an engineering standpoint I'd call this one done."

"Those are good words indeed," smiled Amanda. "If you're confident just call in your people then put some thought into teaching a few basics to some of the Igen folk. I'll check in with Linsey and Ebony to see how they're getting on."

Moira nodded then left the office smiling. She was more than happy to get off Igen permanently. Now just to wait for Reacher to return so she could get back to her own engine room.

While Moira returned to Orca's engine room to confer with Dorind and to gather her team and equipment they heard the general announcement. "Attention all hands, Reacher Fleet is returning. Reacher return expected in nine hours."

"Good news indeed," smiled Moira.

At that announcement, Amanda smiled with delight. "With Moira finished over there I expect we'll soon be on our way. I'll go check in with the rest of my team." With that she left the office in search of Captain Linsey da Silva. She found her in the cargo bay aboard her own ship. "Hello the ship, permission to come aboard?"

"Granted and welcome, Vice-Admiral," grinned Linsey. "We're just hanging around waiting for the learning cycle to finish up."

Amanda glanced over to see one of the people from Igen wearing the learning cap and clinging to the rail as the ship's computer upgraded their language skills. "So, how's it going, Linsey?"

"Good, Vice-Admiral. I've got all three languages in the database, plus we've educated eleven of these folks with the ancient language both vocal and written. This gal here wants to be a teacher, take what she learns and share it with all the Gants. Selea is already at work with that in the Growe circle."

"So, do you have more to do here?"

"Not really, Vice-Admiral. I just thought I'd keep going until everybody else was ready to move on."

"Good to know, Linsey. Moira has already called it done from a repair point of view, and you're ready to go. I'll check in with Ebony now, see how she's making out. With luck we'll be able to wrap this up and be on our way within a week."

"Good to know," smiled Linsey. "Should I stop after this one or should I continue to educate more of them?"

"Up to you."

"Then I'll stop here and start with the clean- up."

"Clean-up?"

"We've been working this around the clock for days. I'd like to tidy up the ship then give the crew a few days' rest."

Amanda chuckled at that. "Do it, Linsey. Tidy it up then take a break." With that she left the small ship and headed back to her office.

Amanda settled into a chair and reached for her comm. "Amanda to Ebony."

"Here."

"You sound busy, Ebony. Where are you?"

"I'm aboard a shuttle breaking in a new pilot. He's got fast reflexes, but tends to over ...yikes ... Yeah, anyway, he just needs a bit more practice."

"Good to know. How many pilots do they have now?"

"Three I'd trust to fly on their own, two more who just need a bit more time at the helm."

"And that's about all they'll get. They can train as many as they want later. Wrap it up and come in, Ebony. We're about ready to close this one down."

* * * * *

While Amanda continued to scale down their operations for the people of Igen, Tonts and Floo continued to track Jara and his two companions. <Where in the name of Igen is that fool going?> mused

Floo. <There's nothing out this way except open spaces. He'll be too easily seen here.>

"Unless he has access to another hidden pathway,> said Tonts.

<There,> shouted the Ronton as he flung out an arm and pointed. They looked and saw a man disappearing into an open hatch in the wall. As they all rushed to the opening to prevent it from closing, Floo spoke to the Ronton.

<You have learned the ancient language?>

<Linsey thought it best if Sen Keta had someone to talk to as that is needed to keep the language in the mind. Sen Tonts is often busy elsewhere, but I'm usually close by.>

<That makes sense,> said Floo as he leaped at the opening and poked his head inside then swiftly withdrew. A spear whistled past him and clattered to the floor. He looked again then stepped inside followed closely by Tonts.

They followed the tunnel for a long time, carefully peering around each bend before proceeding. The lights of Igen dimmed and still they had not found their quarry.

They did find something else useful. Actually, it was Keta's Ronton who noticed the diagram on the wall, partially hidden by the moss growing there. He began to pull it away. <What are you doing? Stop playing about and hurry.>

<No Sen Tonts, look. I can understand the message here, so can you.>

Tonts glanced at it then began to help him clear the moss away. <You're right. Floo, look at this.>

Floo looked for a moment then grinned widely. <Well now, this is useful. We now have a map of these tunnels. These flashing lights here must be the four of us, and those three here must be our quarry.> He clapped the Ronton on the shoulder. <Well done, my friend. Well done indeed. Now we can track that traitor.>

It soon became clear they could track him, but catching him was another matter. Jara had obviously been exploring these tunnels and knew where he was going, they didn't. Slowly the lights of Igen dimmed and fatigue claimed them.

The War's Finally Over

As the lights dimmed on Igen, the fleet returned, the operations were shifted back to Reacher then everyone went to their rest. Rayla was waiting nervously at Twelve's quarters, but she didn't appear to be coming. "Aw, crap, I'll bet she drew the night shift again. Guess I'll have to go down there." She rose and stepped to the door then shrieked and leaped back as it suddenly slid open.

Twelve stood there, grinning at her. "Oops, did I scare you?"

"Stop grinning at me and hug me, hug me now."

"With pleasure, my precious girl. Did you miss me?"

"You know I did and now you're just fishing." Rayla stopped any further discussion by locking her lips on Twelve's. This time there was no hesitation on the SUVI's part, she welcomed the embrace and the intimacy.

"Wow, that held promise," breathed Rayla as their lips slowly parted. "Can we have that conversation now?"

"Shut up and kiss me again," said Twelve as she pulled Rayla tighter to her.

Smiling with delight Rayla raised her lips, but the kiss didn't happen, the comms did. "All Retriever crew to the ship on the double. All Retriever crew to the ship on the double."

"Dammit all to hell and back," snarled Rayla as she reluctantly released her grip on Twelve. "This is getting old. Hold that thought until I get back, my love."

"I'll think of nothing else but your kiss, I promise," sighed Twelve as she released Rayla's hand. "Go on now, duty calls."

With a fast kiss on the cheek for her lover, Rayla fled to the ship, she was the last to arrive. "Stop for another snuggle with a certain SUVI?" grinned Twenty.

"Shut up, Twenty. What's gone sideways on us now? We pulling guard duty again?"

"Something else," said Captain Sessas. "Rebel leader escape through service tunnels, capture Reacher engineer, drag into tunnels. Strikers find, retrieve."

"I heard that. Ready Strikers. Kumar, put us as close as you can."

"Transporting now." He threw the switch and they disappeared from the ship to land beside Floo and Tonts by the entrance to a service tunnel.

* * * * *

While SUVI 12 was enjoying her welcome home kiss, Tonts and Floo led their men along the service tunnels, but found one opened. They peered out into Igen and saw three Gants down with wounds and the prisoner dead. Tonts rushed to them. "What happened? Where's Keta?"

"Jara has her," gasped one of the wounded men. "He appeared out of the wall and struck without warning. They took Keta alive, but ..."

He got no further as Tont's comms spoke from his shoulder. "I have your woman, Tonts. If you want her to remain alive and in one piece you will cease hunting me and break off that disgusting alliance with the Growes. Kill that thing beside you and I'll give back your companion."

Since Jara had no real idea how the comm system worked, he hadn't made a direct call, but had inadvertently sent his message out broadcast to all. Amanda had been giving her report to Jeannie when they heard it.

"Son of a ... Jeannie?"

"Send the strikers to them," said Jeannie as she ran for the transport room with Amanda close behind. I'll go with them. SUVI 5 to SUVI 12."

"Here Five."

"Meet me in Transport, now. We have a hunt."

"Coming."

* * * * *

The strikers arrived to find the Admiral and SUVI 12 already there. Twelve was gazing at an instrument in her hand. Jeannie addressed the strikers. "We have a hunt. Keta has been taken captive by the rebels. Her comm is still active so we can pinpoint her location easy enough. Twelve and I will lead the hunt, you make certain nothing bites us while we do it."

Rayla stepped forward. "Admiral, let us do this. This is what we're trained for, this is what we signed up to do."

Jeannie gazed into her eyes for a moment then relented. "You are correct, the task is yours. Twelve, where are they?"

"They're up one level, but they've made a mistake, they've only got one way out from there if we block the exit at this point." She was tapping the map on her screen, making sure Rayla could see it clearly. She passed over the instrument then Rayla led her troops out. SUVI 20 winked at Twelve as she followed Rayla into the service tunnel.

"We'll just hang out here with these guys, Twelve," said Jeannie.

"There's no need to defend your friend Floo from me, Great Leader," sighed Tonts. "Floo is an ally and a friend. I will not submit to the demands of a madman, nor will I attack a friend."

Floo chuckled at that. "I seem to be making a lot of friends these days. First the one who felled me with a single blow wants to defend me, then the man who has tried for years to kill me says I'm completely safe with him."

"It must be your charming personality," grinned SUVI 12.

"That must be it," replied Floo, matching her grin.

"Actually, I think it was the meat," said Tonts. "I expected to have a difficult time convincing my people to accept the truce with the Growes, but your sudden gift of food, including meat, made the difference. Most agreed they would be happy to defend your people if there were food to be had without a fight to the death."

"That was Selea's idea, she and Eelee. They convinced me to give your people the last of what we had in hopes it would do just that. Fortunately, the Outsiders are exceptional hunters, and we didn't starve after all."

"You gave us the last of what you had? Why?"

"To build the alliance, Tonts. Amanda was quite right all along, unless we work together we'll all perish anyway."

"Agreed." Tonts sighed again and let his gaze wander to the open hatchway to the service tunnel.

* * * * *

As the strikers entered the service tunnel Rayla passed the tracking device back to SUVI 20 who grinned. "Left at the next junction." Rayla nodded and signaled. Young Tomo slipped past her, paused at the junction then leaped around the corner. A moment later his arm reappeared and signaled. They moved forward.

"Next right," said Twenty. This time Rayla went first; the path was clear. "There's the hatch. They're still in here and that's their only way out that I can see on this schematic."

"Understood," said Rayla. "Elke and Tomo, stay here, keep them sealed up. If any of them get past us, make sure they don't escape."

"Understood Commander Mills."

"Let's go. Where are they Twenty?"

"Next left and ahead about ten meters."

Rayla nodded and led out. As she stepped around the corner a spear was thrust at her chest, but she batted it aside and lashed out with her baton. The man staggered back holding his head. Rayla shifted from the baton to the blaster and fired. He went tumbling over backwards and lay still against the wall.

A second man leaped at them, but met the same fate from the blaster. A single man was left standing, holding a struggling woman in his arms. He had a wicked looking blade at her throat. "Stay back, Outsider, or I'll kill her. Your precious servant Tonts won't like that."

Rayla stopped and slowly, carefully returned the blaster to the clip on her belt. As she did, she made eye contact with Keta, then looked at the floor. The second time she did it, Keta nodded that she understood, then went limp and fell to the deck.

Startled, Jara took a step back and looked down at her. When he brought his eyes back up Rayla was on him. Her fist cracked against his jaw, staggering him back. His attempted counter blow was seized in a strong hand, his arm twisted painfully, and he was flipped through the air to land heavily. Before he could get breath back into his lungs, his hands were in restraints behind his back.

"Strike force to Admiral Sorenson."

"Here."

"Success, Admiral. Returning with captives."

"Well done, Rayla, well done."

They soon returned with the three captives. Keta ran into Tonts' arms and he held her tightly. "Are you all right, dear Keta?"

"I'll be fine, Tonts, I will."

"What will you do with the prisoners, Great Leader?" asked Tonts.

"They're not mine to deal with, Tonts, they're all yours."

At that Tonts nodded then moved with startling speed. There was the sound of a smack, and then a grunt as Jara sank to the ground, a blade through his chest. "You've put your hands on Keta twice, traitor, and you have nearly caused the end of our people. We are well rid of you at last."

Still holding Keta close, he turned to the other two. "What will it be? Will you obey the new laws, or would you rather join Jara in the mystery?"

They looked at each other then hung their heads. "We will obey, Sen Tonts."

"Cut them loose, unless Floo has an issue here."

"These are your people, Tonts; they are yours to deal with, but I do approve of your action. The war is now over, and we can get on with the task of survival without fear of each other."

"Then, our job is done here," said Suvi-jean. "Strikers, return to your ship. Twelve, let's go home."

"Before you go, Great Leader," said Keta's Ronton as he stepped forward, "may I speak?"

"Ask your master," came the cold reply.

"Given," said Keta.

"Great Leader, you once asked me if I serve Sen Keta by my own choice or was the choice made for me by another. The answer is both. As a youth I trained with the others, each of us vying for a place as a Ronton, a protector. Once chosen as Ronton, we wait until we are selected to serve and protect a special Sen. I was honored to be chosen by Sen Tonts to protect his beloved. So, the first choice was mine, and then Sen Tonts."

Jeannie sighed and allowed her shoulders to relax. "When I was young I was forced to serve and endured much before I rebelled and won my freedom. I feared it was the same for you. It is a joy to know you were given the option."

Keta stepped closer. "Great Leader, when we first met you suddenly withdrew from me and appointed Amanda to the task of helping us. Was this because you believed I had somehow forced my protector to do what he does, that he would be unwilling if given the choice?"

"It was, Keta. I see I have wronged you, but in my own defense, I believe Amanda has done a better job of it than I would have anyway."

"All your people have been an immense help to us, and we're grateful," she smiled.

"You're welcome. Now, I believe there is still much to do, so I'll leave you to it. Come, Twelve, let's go home." She called for transport and they vanished in a flash of light.

* * * * *

SUVI 12 returned to her quarters to find Rayla waiting for her. "Shut off your comm."

"What?"

"Shut off the damn comm, Twelve, otherwise something else will ..."

"Understood," chuckled Twelve as she took off her tunic and shut off the comm. "Now, come over here and pick up where you left off."

"Where I left off?" asked Rayla, a grin of mischief playing at her lips.

She suddenly shrieked as Twelve leaped across the room and swept her into an embrace. "Didn't anyone ever warn you not to tease a SUVI?"

"Nope, but they should have. So, you caught me, SUVI hunter, what are you going to do with me?"

"Hug you," breathed Twelve as she pulled her closer. "Kiss you and more."

"Mmm, sounds like fun. Tell me about more."

"That'll be up to you to do," whispered Twelve as she inhaled deeply of her lover's scent.

"Twelve?"

"I know what you want from me, and I want that too. The thing is, I'm too scared, I have bad reactions to touch, I don't know what to do to please you, and I'm scared of messing this up. This hunt is yours now, my precious girl. I won't fight you, but you'll have to be patient with me as I learn what you need from me."

"I will, honey, I promise, but what about what you need?"

"Same thing, I just need to learn how ..."

Rayla stopped her with a kiss, then led her to the bed. The comms may have pinged, the small ships might have launched without them, but they were unaware of anything except each other. By the beginning of the next shift Twelve had faced a lot of old fears and learned a bunch of exciting new things.

Rayla smiled as Twelve snuggled closer in her sleep. She lightly kissed her forehead and whispered, "There now, that didn't hurt after all, did it?" She smiled with delight and closed her eyes.

Wrapping It Up

For the next five days a number of Reacher's crew worked with the folk of Igen on the bridge and other stations, teaching, guiding, and making friends in the process. When they felt certain they could do no more there was a gathering of the people involved in the Reacher's briefing room. Tonts and Keta were there as well as Floo, Eelee, and Selea.

"Looks like we're all here," smiled Jeannie. "Vice-Admiral Drake, the meeting is yours."

Amanda stood and spoke. "All right, let's begin. I believe we've accomplished as much as we can here. Moira, report."

"Aye, Vice-Admiral. We've repaired as many of Igen's systems as we could, rerouted a few more, stabilized the main reactor, got the engines back on line, and taught as much engineering to the folk as we could in such a short time. However, they're clever people and they have all the instruction manuals. Unless we plan to stay a few more years I'd say we've done all we can from an engineering standpoint."

"Linsey, report."

"I've managed to get three new languages into my database. We've learned the history of how the people of Igen came to be and made that available to them, we managed to get fourteen in all educated in both spoken and written language of the elder race, the builders of Igen. Four have taken on the task of teaching the rest of the folk what they've learned. I believe I'm finished."

"Ebony?"

"They have five shuttles useful and four competent pilots for them. It's done from that angle."

"Tonts, are you satisfied we've done what we can? Are you confident your people are ready?"

Tonts looked to Floo who nodded. He turned back to Amanda. "We are more than satisfied with all your people have done for us, Amanda. You have saved Igen for future generations, nurtured her

175

back to health and put her on a course to a place of hope for those generations.

"More, you have managed to stop the war between us, shown us a better way, and as a result we will survive. I cannot imagine what more you could possibly do."

"Well, there is one thing more you could do," said Floo, grinning.

"What is that, Floo?"

"You could leave us a few of those SUVI hunters."

Amanda laughed at that. "Sorry, Floo, but we're keeping our SUVI hunters."

"Then I agree with Tonts, you've done far more than we could have imagined. We have no way to properly thank you for all you've managed, but I promise you this. Voices will be raised in song of your visit, and the young to come will learn those songs. You will be remembered through the generations as long as the people of Igen continue to survive."

"As will you, Floo. We have made many friends here, and they will be remembered fondly. Come, Captains Tonts and Floo, we will accompany you to transport then wish you a safe journey."

They reached the transportation area to find SUVI 12 and Rayla waiting for them. Twelve was holding a gleaming sharp spear. She stepped toward Floo and spoke. "A hunter needs a good spear. I seem to recall I broke your last one." She smiled as she passed it to him.

"Yes, over my head as I remember it. Thank you, great hunter, I will cherish the gift and the offer of friendship." She smiled and stepped back as they stood on the transport pads then vanished.

Jeannie sighed and turned to Amanda. "Well done, my love. You accomplished so much more than I could have. I should make you the admiral."

"Forget that, Suvi-jean. I know you're building another small ship. You're not saddling me with all the work while you run off to play."

"It was worth a shot," chuckled Jeannie. "All right, call a full captain's meeting plus passenger reps. Let's put this one to rest then be on our way."

With a twinkle in her eye, Amanda put out the call.

"Looks like we're all here, Admiral."

"Thank you Vice-Admiral. Well, people, it looks like we're done here. Amanda, report. How did we do?"

"We managed to repair most of the alien ship, Admiral. We also managed to stop the war between her peoples, teach them how to run the ship, at least learn how to run it, set them on a new course toward a planet where they can survive, gained more languages for Linsey's database, and the admiral got a chance to go hunting.

"Sadly, we took two serious injuries, but both people will eventually return to full duty. That's about it."

"So you're ready to call it?"

"I am, Admiral. We've done as much as we can do here. I say it's time to move on."

"I agree," said Jeannie. "Anybody else got any reason to hang around here halfway between star systems?"

There was a round of chuckles and Nos. "Very well then, Captain Moore, aim us at the next star system. We'll take one last quick look at it then move on from there. Captains return to your ships and prepare to move out."

An hour later Jeannie and Amanda walked onto the bridge of the Reacher. "Captain Moore, are we ready?"

"Aye, Admiral. The fleet is ready and awaiting your order; the table in Simple Pleasures is set and awaiting our arrival."

"Then let's get on the go. Fleet ahead three quarter speed."

* * * * *

On the bridge of Igen Floo and Tonts stood side by side watching the screen as the three bright dots beside Igen winked out. "There they go, Tonts. We're on our own now. What will you do first?"

"First I want to go see how Keta and Selea are doing with that school they're setting up, and then I want to settle in to read the log of the first captain, see if I can get a sense of what he hoped to accomplish. What about you, Floo? What will you do first?"

"I think I'll go hunting, test out this new spear the SUVI hunter gave me."

"Let me know how it goes," grinned Tonts as he walked away.

"I will. Shall we meet at first light tomorrow and start making real plans?"

"Agreed, Floo. At first light. Good hunting."

"I'll bring you some meat," chuckled Floo as he trotted away towards Eelee and the waiting trees of Igen.

* * * * *

As they sat around chatting over too many desserts, Jeannie noticed the faraway look in Amanda's eye. "Thinking about our friends on Igen?"

"Yeah, I am actually. Just hoping they can keep the dream alive through enough generations to reach a safe haven. Ah well, we did our best for them, it's in their hands now."

"Mandy, I say again, you did an amazing job on this one. You sure you don't want the top job?"

"Forget it, Suvi-jean. No, I just did it the way you'd do it. Figure out where the blockages are and find the right person to fix them, then stand back and let them work. These folks really wanted a solution, and they stepped up to make it happen. I'm rather proud of them."

"And I'm exceptionally proud of you."

"Thank you, and forget it, I'm not taking on your job while you go play."

"It was worth a shot," chuckled Jeannie.

* * * * *

While the admiral and friends indulged themselves at Simple Pleasures, SUVI 12 lay snuggled in Rayla's arms. "Well, my precious girl, we're interstellar, not likely to get interrupted by the comms."

"I suppose not," grinned Rayla. "How do you suggest we spend our time?"

"I think we should review the lessons."

"Review the lessons?"

"Yes, the lessons you taught me last night. I confess I was keeping close track of the procedure until the end, then I seem to have lost all memory of what was done."

"Lost all memory of the lessons?"

"Yes. You did something and my mind exploded. When I got my wits back I couldn't remember a single thing. You'll have to teach me all over again."

"Oh dear, well then, I guess we'll have to start at the beginning if you've forgotten everything."

"I forgot it all," grinned Twelve, "every last detail. Start at the beginning."

"With extreme pleasure," purred Rayla as she pulled Twelve closer and kissed her. Twelve's only response was a groan of pleasure and a silent prayer that the trip to the next system would take days.

The End

And now for a peek at the final story in the Forgotten Worlds series:

Ten

by

Prudence MacLeod

Mariena

A soft wind sighed around the decaying buildings and tall structures long since abandoned. Little grew in this area, so most creatures avoided the places of the past occupation. Long ago the people who built the now empty cities left Mariena to explore beyond, but they never returned. Only those who'd served them, and fought them, defeated them, remained.

They were fewer now, the Marienas, and only shadows of what they once were. Whether habit or tradition is not known, but the Marienas always looked to the sky each night. Were they looking for the Gorthas to return, or were they hoping they wouldn't? No matter, the night sky always smiled down on them, until ...

Brainstorming

It's the same in every society, and so it is on the ships of the Wandering Fleet. The explorers and other great commanders, the leaders and heroes do what they do, but they in turn depend on others. The others, the unsung heroes who grow, gather, and prepare the food then clean up after; the cleaners who keep the quarters and corridors clean, those who store and catalogue the supplies, and so on.

For the greats and mighty to do what they do they depend on others to keep things running smoothly, and yet these people have lives too, lives of hope, struggle, success, and failure, of need and fulfilment. Here are a few of those and how they interplay with the greats of the fleet as their combined peoples struggle for survival.

* * * * *

The small fleet of survivors sped through interstellar space on its way toward the next star system they planned to explore. On the home ship, Reacher, a brawl had broken out in the passenger's recreation area between the crews of Orca and Retriever. A few of the SUVI had been enjoying a time of peace together when it happened. As one they rose and waded in, trying to break up the fight before Security forces arrived.

Rayla Mills, commander of Retriever's strike force, found herself being held back by SUVI 20. "Rayla, Rayla, cut it out, calm down."

"Let me go and get the hell out of my way, Twenty."

"Nope, can't do it. Rayla, that was too close, you might have killed him. Get a grip. Here comes Security, just go with them, and don't make a fuss."

"That bastard pulled a knife ..."

"And you broke his arm. Nineteen has his buddies under control, it's over. Deep breaths. Atta girl, now make nice with Security and I'll find Twelve, let her know what happened."

Rayla nodded and allowed the officer to lead her to the brig. The rest of her strike force was there, as were several of the Orca crew with SUVI 19 watching carefully. "All right, men of Orca crew, stay here and I'll come for you in the morning. Right now, I have to go back and smooth this over with the President of the Passenger's Association." With that Nineteen strode away. Several onlookers watched as the unconscious man was carefully lifted onto a stretcher and wheeled away to the infirmary.

* * * * *

The next morning, as the wounded man slowly regained his senses and realized where he was, two women sat in an office chatting; perhaps brain storming might be a better word. The first was Antha, an Earalithian woman, small of stature as are all her species, and yet exceptionally clever and tenacious. The second was Ebony Graves, a young woman from a failed human colony who had risen dramatically to a command post within the fleet.

Ebony sighed with delight as she finished her tea and set down the cup. "I'm still a bit puzzled."

"Oh? About what?"

"About Igen. I mean, why didn't we just transport those people over to Reacher and adopt them into the fleet, or at least drop them off at the planet. Why leave them on a dying ship?"

Antha smiled. "Ebony, our leaders are so wise. I had a few thoughts on this and asked the vice-admiral about it. She said we couldn't do that at first, they were in the middle of a war and extremely savage. They'd have torn Reacher apart in their desire to make an end of each other.

"Once we got them working together it was easy to see. Their understanding of their reason to exist was to nurture Igen, their religion if you will. Removing them from that ship would be like ripping a babe from the arms of its mother.

"We helped them stop the war and taught them how to care for Igen, that was the motivation for both sides. Now that they have a greater understanding of their situation, they can regain much of their lost knowledge, and yet have a few generations to prepare themselves to abandon that ship, to progress to the next step of their evolution.

"Yes, we've adopted others into the fleet, but each of those groups were already space farers, aware of what we are and what we're trying to do. Those folks on Igen weren't ready for that step, we dared not separate them from their god, the giver and sustainer of life."

"Wow. When you look at it like that, it does make sense," sighed Ebony. "That also makes Captain Sessas even more remarkable in how she's managed to adapt."

"Indeed it does."

Ebony drained the last of her tea then grinned. "So, are you ready to tell me what's on your mind yet?"

Antha smiled. "Can't fool you, can I? Okay, Ebony, I'll talk. I recently discovered something intriguing in the ship's archives. It's something the humans once experimented with in an attempt to help people of diverse backgrounds interact with, and become more comfortable with, each other."

"Okay, so you like this idea, whatever it was, and you think it has possible applications for the fleet. You want to run it past me before taking it to the admiral."

"You know me too well," chuckled Antha. "We're interstellar now, and as ship's counselor, I'm always a lot busier when we're between adventures. Interstellar is boring for you action addicts."

Ebony laughed at that. "Yeah, it can be, all right. So, tell me more, what's the idea?"

"A living library."

"Explain please."

"A living library, a place where I can send a client to help them get more comfortable with other species. It would be manned with volunteers from every species we have in the fleet, human, Earalith, SUVI, Morar, Maccay, and with luck I'll be able to talk Captain Sessas into it as well."

"Okay, so what do these volunteers do there?"

"They talk to the people who come in to talk to them. Like this, you're a human but you struggle a bit with having the Morar around, something about them puts you off. Your therapist, me, has sent you there to meet one and talk to them. The volunteer sits down and talks with you."

"About?"

"Anything at all. The idea is to help you see the volunteer as a person, another living being much like yourself, different in appearance, yes, but underneath the surface differences, the same, just another person trying to survive as best they can, to find joy and meaning in life as are we all. What do you think?"

"Wow, Antha, I think this has a world of potential, but you'll have to be careful who you choose for volunteers, and who you send to them."

"I know. Please understand, I won't send anyone there unless they ask to go. I'll tell them about it but let them make that decision for themselves. Once I'm sure they're ready and want to go, I'll arrange it."

"Sounds good, but I'd add a bit to it, make it more fun."

"Oh? How can we make it more fun?"

"Get lots of volunteers. Picture this, I walk into your living library. A woman greets me there. I say I'm there to talk to a SUVI. She shows me three options, one is a SUVI hunter, another an intuitive, and yet the other something else again. I choose one and they put us together with tea and snacks. I bet I could talk Alli into catering for it."

Antha smiled and sat back in her chair; Ebony shook a finger at her. "Oh, don't look so smug. You knew darn well you'd be able to hook me into running with this thing."

"It's a natural for you, Ebony. Helping people find their place is your passion, and this has Ebony Graves stamped all over it. What do you say, you want to give it a go?"

"You know I do. Okay, first I need to talk to the president of the passenger's association, get her on side and score some space, then I need to call in a few favors to get it set up. Actually, I think I need to run this past the Admiral and Captain Moore, get their take on it.

"Your job will be to point me toward a few likely volunteers. I'll find others and send them to you. You can interview them before we put them to work or not, make sure they're a good fit." She rose to her feet with a smile of anticipation. "Okay, I'm off to track down the admiral."

* * * * *

Meanwhile, the admiral was in a meeting with the captains of the fleet. Suvi-jean Sorenson, Admiral of the Wandering Fleet, was pacing about as usual, trying to calm and organize her thoughts. The captains sat waiting; they'd seen her like this before. Finally, the vice-admiral, Amanda Drake, Suvi-jean's bonded companion and second in command of the fleet, took pity on the others and spoke.

"Admiral?"

"Huh? Oh, sorry people. Yes, I called you here to deal with a growing problem. Things can get a bit out of hand when we're interstellar. Bored people can make mistakes, get up to mischief, and worse. Recently I've noticed a growing issue of racism among the crews. Captain Moore, report."

Rhonda Moore, captain of the Reacher, sighed and nodded. "Aye, Admiral. It happened again last night, another brawl in the passenger area. This time it got a bit ugly. A couple of men from Orca crew started blowing off about the uselessness of having Retriever still active, saying they'd be better able to do the job.

"It went to hell when they made a few nasty remarks about the Retriever's captain. Rayla Mills decked one and the war was on. SUVIs Nine, Sixteen, Nineteen, and Twenty waded in to break it up before Security got there."

"Dammit," snarled Sheila Singh, captain of the Orca, "I'll deal with those fools. Did you get their names?"

"One's in the brig," replied Rhonda, "the other is in medical under guard, Nineteen picked up the rest."

"Medical?"

"Apparently, he pulled a knife on Rayla Mills. She broke him up pretty bad, would have killed him if Twenty hadn't pulled her off."

"Is she in the brig too?" asked the Admiral.

"No longer. She spent the night there cooling off for throwing the first punch, but I won't punish a woman for defending herself. We cut her loose this morning."

"You did right, Rhonda," said Jeannie, and Sheila nodded her agreement. "All right, people, we need to do something about this. It's been happening more and more when we're between systems. I'm wide open to suggestions here."

"Can't force folk to like folk," said Sessas, captain of the Retriever and the only Saurian in the entire fleet. "Try, make worse." That brought a round of agreement from the rest.

"Any suggestions Sessas?" asked Jeannie.

"Ask Antha, Ebony, maybe have idea."

"Good thinking, Captain Sessas," nodded Jeannie, reaching for her comm. "Commander Ebony Graves to the bridge briefing room. Repeat, Commander Ebony Graves to the bridge briefing room."

"On my way, Admiral," came the response from Jeannie's shoulder pin.

"While we wait for her to arrive, I have another suggestion. Sheila, I understand yours is the main war ship, and I know you've molded that crew into an efficient unit, a ship of warriors. Now you need to go to the next step."

"Make those hardheaded fools understand the rest of the population is who we're defending, keeping safe. They will never feel safe, fully trust us, if this crap keeps happening. I understand, Jeannie, and I've been working on it. I'll admit I could use help with this. I'm wide open to suggestions."

"I have one," said Hal White, Security Chief for the Reacher and commander of the fighter ship, EX4.

"Let's hear it, Hal," said Sheila.

"Give the job to Nineteen. When the admiral first arrived on the Reacher I was wearing the same attitude those guys are. I was armed and in full armor, yet she beat the snot out of me, removing the ego issue. In the days and weeks that followed I saw how she used her superior abilities to nurture and protect the rest of us, not go on an ego trip showing off her superiority."

Sheila nodded. "Nineteen huh? Why not. I'll see what he has to say about it."

At that point Ebony arrived. "You called for me, Admiral?"

"Indeed we did, Ebony. Please, sit down. Now here's the problem we want your input with."

As she sat listening, Ebony's grin grew wider. "I see. Admiral, I was actually looking for you to run an idea past you. Antha got me interested in this earlier today, but I wanted your input and permission before running with it." She continued to outline the idea of a living library for them.

When she finished Jeannie nodded. "I get it, Ebony. It's a lot harder to feel superior to someone who you know personally and like. If we can get some of the more troublesome types involved with this it could be a big help. What do you think, Captains?"

"I like it," said Captain Baris, Jeannie's grandfather, and captain of the salvage ship Recovery Two.

"I once visited such a place on old Earth," smiled Olga Volkov, captain of Recovery One. "It was indeed an eye-opening experience."

Rhonda Moore smiled as she spoke. "I like it. I say set it up then we send some of our tough characters for a visit."

"Can't," said Captain Sessas.

"Why not, Sessas?" asked Sheila.

"Is punishment. Make angrier, blame victim, blame you, resent everybody. Must decide to go themselves. They go, they learn, share with others on crew. Much better."

"She's right," said Ebony. "You can tell them about it, suggest they might give it a try, but no more. They'll have to go to Antha and ask to go."

"Each step is a step forward," sighed Jeannie. "Do it, Ebony. Let us know when you're ready for visitors."

"Thank you, Admiral. With your permission I'll be about the task." At Jeannie's nod Ebony rose and left the room.

* * * * *

While Ebony sought out her companion, Ensign Brie Elliot, and explained the new project, the Marienas came out to gaze at the sky. Suddenly, as one, they turned their gaze toward a new direction, a new part of the sky near the horizon. Something, or someone, was coming.

"Are they returning, do you think?" The question ran through the assembly of creatures as they faced the new direction.

"Perhaps, but more likely something new. We should let them explore while we observe, explore the possibilities, test them, find the weaknesses, and then destroy them, send them away never to return."

A general humming sound of agreement was heard. "Hmmmmm."

"We will not serve them."

"No, that we will not do, but we will test them, find the weaknesses, drive them out never to return." Again the hum of general consensus sounded over the landscape. They searched the memories left to them by the ancestors, seeking and reviewing the methods of testing, clouding the mind of another creature while inflicting damage to the being's systems, searching out weaknesses, judging their worth, preparing for the battle of survival, of dominance.

Don't miss out!

Visit the website below and you can sign up to receive emails whenever Prudence MacLeod publishes a new book. There's no charge and no obligation.

https://books2read.com/r/B-A-ZKBBB-MCHRC

BOOKS 2 READ

Connecting independent readers to independent writers.

Also by Prudence MacLeod

Forgotten Worlds
Suvi
Echo of the Past
Survivors
Ship
Fleet
Unite
IGEN

Watch for more at https://www.prudencemacleod.com/.

Telling a story is like knitting a sweater. Start with a ball of possibilities, pull out one small thread and begin. With luck and patience you will create something quite wonderful.

About the Author

On a far off windswept island Jennifer Crandall sits with her dogs and cats creating fantastic stories for all to enjoy. She publishes as JL Crandall, Prudence MacLeod, and Jenni Leigh.

Read more at https://www.prudencemacleod.com/.

www.ingramcontent.com/pod-product-compliance
Lightning Source LLC
Chambersburg PA
CBHW020954180626
46814CB00003B/1092